MW00934964

Commander to Crown
Lessons Learned as a Naval Officer, Orthodontist, and Beauty Queen

Dr. Corinne Devin

Copyright © 2022 by Dr. Corinne Devin
Cover Design Copyright © 2022 by Dr. Corinne Devin
All Rights Reserved.

Author:
Dr. Corinne Devin

Title:
Commander to Crown: Lessons Learned as a Naval Officer, Orthodontist, and Beauty Queen

Rights:
All rights reserved. This book or any portion thereof may not be reproduced or used in any manner whatsoever without the express written permission of the author, except for the use of brief quotations in a book review.

For more information, visit DrCorinneDevin.com

Disclaimers:
Names may have been changed to protect privacy. The views expressed in this publication are those of the author and do not necessarily reflect the official policy or position of the Department of Defense or the U.S. government.

The public release clearance of this publication by the Department of Defense does not imply Department of Defense endorsement or factual accuracy of the material.

Printed:
In the United States of America

First Edition:
April 2022

ISBN:
9798826996676

PRAISE FOR *COMMANDER TO CROWN*

"As a 5x published author, speaker, podcast host, and life coach, I recognize when I read a story that can be a source of power for others. Corinne's book delivers not only her story but also motivating and actionable advice that lays the example and blueprint to help any woman (or man) achive more — personally, emotionally, and professionally.

I know that Corinne's stories and philosophies can change lives, because she has changed mine."

Laurel House
- Celebrity Relationship and Empowerment Coach
- As seen on *Today, KTLA, E!, Good Morning America, Vogue, O, Cosmopolitan, Thrillist, Self Magazine, BravoTV, Woman's Day, AskMen, Glamour,* and *Readers Digest*

"I know first-hand the story Corinne shares will not only impact you but motivate you for greatness. She has a wealth of knowledge when it comes to making the impossible possible, and her book and engaging storytelling style gives you the skills to get there."

Theresa Carpenter
- Leader, Storyteller, and Advocate
- Naval Officer, Published Author, Podcast Host, and Public Relations Officer

DEDICATION

This book is dedicated to my mentors, professors, fellow Junior League sisters, and all the people in my life who pushed me, challenged me, and believed in me.

TABLE OF CONTENTS

INTRODUCTION

On September 9, 2009, I landed back in San Diego with my Navy dental team to start our post-deployment training and to get some much-needed rest. The perfect 75-degree weather felt like absolute paradise after nine months in Iraq with below-zero temperatures in January and over 130-degree temperatures in July and August.

Three weeks later, I flew to Austin, Texas to compete in the United America pageant. My military colleagues couldn't believe I was entering another pageant.

Even my own parents asked disapprovingly, "Why are you doing this? How is a pageant going to help your career?"

No one was supportive of my decision to compete. They all saw it as a waste of time, talent, and money. For a moment, I questioned myself too. I hadn't worn high heels in almost a year. So, to go from full combat gear to shiny ball gowns seemed foreign to me.

"Snap out of it," I said to myself gently. "Remember what matters."

I love serving my country. I love being a dentist. But I also love competing in pageants. Why choose one when I can excel in all three?

I took a deep breath and refocused my mind on my ability to adapt, maintain poise, and project confidence when walking on stage and speaking in my interviews with the judges.

As soon as I arrived to check in, however, I immediately felt out of place. Every day for the past 10 months I wore the exact same military-issued fatigues and stood quickly at attention when someone walked in the room. Now I was squeezing into colorful dresses, wearing makeup, and doing my best to not trip in high heels.

Before I knew it, I was on stage under bright lights. It was now down to the top three contestants to answer a pivotal question.

I was one of them.

"Corinne, as someone who just returned from Iraq, how do you feel about President Obama sending 70,000 troops to Afghanistan?" asked the host, sticking a microphone in front of my mouth and smiling slyly toward the audience.

Everyone's eyes were on me. I tried not to show any reaction on my face, but it was hard to hold back a gasp. I was stunned. Why was I being asked this? Usually, religious and political questions were off-limits in pageants. I knew that this question should not be asked. It was inappropriate.

Yet, the emcee must have thought he could outsmart me. He wanted to test my ability to answer a delicate question under pressure and see if he could throw me off balance.

The stakes were high. If I didn't answer it, I would lose the competition and the crown, but if I did answer it and mistakenly say something in a way that appeared to undermine my military leadership, I would violate the Uniform Code of Military Justice.

I took a calm breath, smiled, and looked at the judges.

"Yes, you are right that President Obama is shifting the Operation from Iraq to Afghanistan. As a proud member of the military, I know that if we can show the Afghan people acts of selfless service— helping the local people with no expectations of anything in return, like we did in Iraq, which is felt in the core of our beliefs as Americans—then we are doing our job. God bless those troops."

I didn't know the political views or biases of the judges, but that didn't matter anyhow. I wanted to answer truthfully to reflect who I was and what I believed.

Five minutes later, I was crowned Ms. United America 2009.

Five days later, I was back at Marine Corps Air Station Miramar finishing post-deployment training.

(President and Emcee of the 2019 Mrs./Ms. Earth Pageant, Mykhael Michaels, asking me the onstage question at the South Point Hotel, Las Vegas, Nevada — Photo by Intuition Design Photography)

A NOTE FROM THE AUTHOR

Thank you for picking up this book. Hopefully you were intrigued by the introductory story to hear more about my life and lessons learned with a unique overlap of passions: dentistry, serving as a leader in the military, and competing in pageants.

This book is broken into 13 chapters. Each of the first 12 chapters begins with a visual timeline, showing some important events that are discussed in that chapter, and ends with some advice I'd love to share with you based on my life experiences from that stage in my journey.

In Chapter 13, you will find some inspiration, parting words, and even actionable activities. They are written for anyone who has ever felt inferior, discouraged, or lost in life.

Nobody's journey is smooth and linear. We all stumble, we all have setbacks, and we all have obstacles that we encounter in our personal and professional lives.

Challenges, failure, and learning all happen.

Welcome and embrace it all.

"The key to success is to start before you are ready." —Marie Forleo

I hope you enjoy reading.

Corinne

Commander, United States Navy
Orthodontist, Diplomate of American Board of Orthodontics
Ms. Earth 2018

CHAPTER 1: WHERE I STARTED

Timeline
Chapter 1

1981
On February 10, I was born on a US naval base in the Philippines.

In August, we moved to California.

1984
My brother Nicholas was born in April at Long Beach Naval Hospital.

1988
In January, we moved to Kailua, Hawaii.

I almost drowned in the pool.

1989
We moved onto the base in Kaneohe Bay, Hawaii.

I almost drowned in the ocean.

1990
After my first day of 4th grade, my mom, crying, told me my dad deployed to Saudi Arabia for Operation Desert Storm.

We spent Christmas in Miami without my dad.

1991
My dad returned home in March.

In August, we moved to Manteca, California, and I started 5th grade.

1993
I entered 7th grade with contacts and a perm.

1995
I tried out for Manteca High School cheerleading, made it, but couldn't join because we moved again -- to Reno, Nevada.

1999
I graduated from Galena High School in Reno, ready to start at St. Mary's College in the Fall.

On February 10, 1981, I was born at the United States Naval Base Subic Bay in the Philippines, where my father was stationed and working as a dentist. My mother had been told she was having twins, but as she and my father welcomed me into the world, it was only me.

Although it's too bad I didn't get the unique experience of having a twin, I was lucky to be born into a navy family with seven generations of service dating back to the Revolutionary War. Serving our country runs strong in my family. My father was a Lieutenant in the Navy, and my mother was a former civil servant dental assistant.

We left the Philippines when I was six months old and moved to Huntington Beach, California. We soon moved to Carlsbad and had a house in a cul-de-sac. My brother Nicholas was born three years later at the Long Beach Naval Hospital.

Every day my dad made the 40-minute drive from where we lived to the naval base in San Diego for his year-long fellowship to improve his general dentistry skills. Since my father was gone most of the day, I spent most of my time with my mother, who would take my brother and me to school, the park, the beach, and other fun activities. I didn't understand why my dad worked the hours he did or why he had to commute so far away, but we all loved where we lived.

On the weekends, my dad would work in the yard, and my brother and I loved to help and goof around together. We'd play with the garden hose and get each other wet when the other one wasn't paying attention. I loved being a big sister and thought how fun it would be to throw Nicholas over the stairwell banister. I always wanted to be in charge and did wrestle with some mixed feelings from no longer being the center of attention and having to share everything.

Because I was a very energetic and strong-willed 4-year-old, my parents decided I needed to channel my energy into music. They started me out with a baby violin, a Kawasaki. I drove my teacher Ms. Nakamura nuts. I didn't like to practice because the chin rest would bruise my cheek. Plus, I had super thick glasses like the old

Coca-Cola bottles—they made reading music difficult. Ms. Nakamura was so strident and intense that she drove her husband away and her daughter into a perfect violinist and pianist.

My glasses were a permanent fixture on my face. They had been there ever since I was eight months old to help with my cross-eyes because of accommodative esotropia. I actually grew to love my glasses, although my mother would tell you that I constantly threw them off my face.

After three years in California, we moved to Kailua, Hawaii, in January 1988. I was getting ready to enter 1st grade, and my brother was in preschool. I remember getting off the airplane where we were greeted by leis to wear as necklaces. My parents had found a house with a pool in Kaneohe Bay near the base where my dad was stationed. I loved to swim.

One day I was riding my yellow truck around the pool, and one of the wheels went over the edge. I flipped over right into the pool, but I got stuck in the truck. Luckily, Dad jumped in and pulled me out. To my surprise, he then said, "Wait, this would be perfect for my CPR class I'm teaching next week!"

Dad loved having photos, stories, and real-life examples when it came to teaching. He pushed me back into the pool and told me to do a dead man float in my wet, soggy clothes.

Since he was so excited to capture the teachable moment on film, I forgot how I was feeling. Plus, I was still in shock from nearly drowning, so I didn't really process it. I just played along.

Next, he had me climb out of the pool and lie flat on the cement. My mom came out and saw me in soaked clothing but didn't know what had happened. She nodded silently to see if I was okay; I nodded back. So she didn't protest when my dad instructed her to take photos before and during his CPR demonstration.

A year later, we moved onto the base in Kaneohe Bay. We didn't have a pool anymore, but we had the ocean. Every March, we'd watch the whales go by; even my mom would stop what she was doing to see them. She said we had a million-dollar view. She was right. I loved the ocean but didn't like how the sand would get everywhere and how it rust my swing set. I had to ask Santa Claus each December for the same gift.

But I did love having family visit us, especially when my dad left for a week here and there during his pre-deployment training with the Marines. Seeing my Uncle Peter, my dad's brother, made me feel I still had a piece of my dad there and helped reduce the sadness of missing him a little.

One time when I went down to the beach, I told my brother I wanted to learn how to surf. I figured I could use my boogie board as a surfboard, so I grabbed it and ran straight into the ocean. However, I didn't anticipate the power of the undercurrent and when I tried to stand up, I lost my balance and got taken in by the tide. It was so strong that I couldn't come up for air. I was terrified and don't remember what happened next. I just remember waking up on the beach with my dad leaning over me after performing CPR. He rescued me again. That was the last time I tried surfing, and a new fear was permanently set in me.

In September 1990, now about nine years old, I came home from the first day of 4th grade to see my mother crying at our kitchen table.

She glanced up and said, "Your father left early this morning to go with the Marines to Saudi Arabia for Operation Desert Storm."

Although there had been 10 deployment false alarms over the past two weeks—where we had all gone to the hanger to say goodbye to my dad only to have it postponed again—I was confused. How was he here one day and gone the next?

"Your father and I didn't want to wake you and your brother up and throw off your first day of school, especially if it was another false alarm. We didn't think he'd actually be deployed today," my mom added.

"When will he come home?" I asked.

My mom shook her head despondently. I could tell she was feeling hurt and abandoned. She, like many other moms in my neighborhood, became a single parent overnight.

"You can write to him and President Bush if you want him to come home," was all she said.

Her statement shocked me initially. I could barely write for my school work and the idea of writing the President was beyond me. However, I did like the idea that I could write to my dad as a way to feel close to him. Every month my mom would write a letter and I would add to it. My brother would draw a picture to put inside to show what he was most excited about. It was our only lifeline to my dad during this time.

My first thoughts with having my dad gone were, who would take me to violin lessons? And, who would help my brother and me with karate? I had no idea how long he'd be gone, but I started to understand the meaning and feeling of time—minutes versus days versus months versus years. I was nervous his absence would go on forever.

My next thoughts reflected some maturation. I was better at understanding the idea of choosing between right and wrong, and I realized I needed to look after my younger brother. I felt a stronger sense of responsibility now, and I silently committed to telling the truth and not making up stories to lie about situations like I had when I was younger.

Halloween on base was much different that year because there were so many kids walking around without their fathers or mothers. I was happy that my mom had other parent friends who knew what it was like to have their significant other away.

As my brother and I made our lap around the neighborhood, we stopped at the last house for our night of trick-or-treating. This house didn't have anything at the door but directed people towards the garage instead. My brother and I walked into a maze of sheets. Carrying our pumpkin-shaped candy pails with care, I made sure Nicholas walked behind me. Suddenly, the boogeyman jumped out. I screamed, kicked, and punched him as hard as I could, snatched the candy, grabbed my brother's hand, and ran out fast.

The next day my mom said to me, "Corinne, you need to apologize to our neighbor across the street."

"Why?" I asked in disbelief.

"Well, you kicked and punched him yesterday when you went trick-or-treating."

"No, Mom. I beat up the boogeyman at his house. I *rescued* him."

She shook her head and shrugged since she knew there was no convincing me.

Christmas for my family was very different that year too. My mother, brother, and I flew to Miami to spend time with my Aunt Barbara, Uncle "RE" (who was stationed in the Coast Guard there), and my grandparents (who flew in from California to join us).

My dad sent the best Christmas gifts from abroad, but what I remember most were the postcards of the women making blankets and carpets. Their faces were almost completely covered, and their outfits were black or a print. It made me think of Jasmine, the Arabian princess from the movie Aladdin, and what it would be like on a magic carpet ride.

The day after Christmas, my family decided to go to Walt Disney World in Orlando. Although it was raining, we were not deterred. As we boarded my first-ever roller coaster ride called Space Mountain, my thoughts were not about missing my dad this Christmas, but rather, "What did I just sign up for?"

My brother sat behind me, and my uncle was in front. Right before the ride started, he reached back and yelled, "Are you ready, kids?!"

We shook our heads nervously. *Vroom!*

Throughout the entire ride, my uncle screamed in fear. My brother and I were speechless, gripping the handles for dear life. It was our first adrenaline rush, and we loved every minute of it.

In late March 1991, my dad returned from Saudi Arabia. At only 10 years old, I didn't understand that my father had no control over when he could return, so I was upset that he had missed my birthday in February but made it back in time for my brother's in April. It was hard being the eldest child. I felt like I had to grow up fast while my dad was on deployment, but my brother remained calm and unphased like he was in his own world where time stood still. In some ways, I was envious that he could stay so kid-like.

Initially, it was hard to have my dad around again because we had gotten so used to life without him. It wasn't that we didn't want him back, but it took some adjusting. I was afraid he would leave suddenly again and miss more of my life. At the time I didn't understand what my father did (other than being a dentist) or the sacrifices my family made until I was much older.

There were several times we thought my father was going to leave on deployment again, and each time, my parents would wake me up to say goodbye to my dad, only to then have him come back several hours later. This happened three times. So, on the fourth time, when my dad realized it was no longer a false alarm, he told my mom not to wake up my brother and me.

My family and I went to counseling to work through hurt feelings and readjustment pains. In counseling, I shared how upset I was that I didn't get to say goodbye to him in person the last time he left. It wasn't until I was much older and in the military myself that I truly understood how conflicted my parents were. I finally understood the stress they felt in the constant back and forth of saying goodbye and living in uncertainty. My parents did their best to protect me. Looking back, I am grateful that we took the time to talk things out and how much my parents cared about us.

In August, we left Hawaii and moved to Manteca, California—a farming community near Stockton. Here, my dad would finish his time in the Navy at the Rough and Ready Island Naval Supply Depot before it closed and became part of the Port of Stockton.

My parents and I felt the culture shock immediately upon arrival. We had left the laid-back pace of Hawaii, a comfortable bubble in our own time warp, and dropped into the fast-paced hustle of California, where you felt like you were in a constant state of playing catch up.

After three years away, it felt like we were entering a new country. We were no longer on Hawaiian time, and we lost the safety net of living on a base where you knew everyone and their families in your unit. His command in Kaneohe Bay had been very close-knit—they looked out for each other. He wasn't just a number, but a person and extension of the family; the camaraderie there had been strong as steel.

In California, he didn't feel the same level of depth and connection. It seemed like his boss judged him by a piece of paper without really getting to know him or us. In his first few months, my dad was given an assignment in the middle of nowhere, about a 5-hour drive away. He could only come home on the weekends.

My mom became a single parent overnight again, but this time she didn't have the support system she had in Hawaii. She felt alone and, after the first week of my father's absence, had a meltdown. My dad came home immediately. He had thought my mom could handle the separation well, as she had with Operation Desert Storm, but he was wrong. His bosses agreed to take him off the rotation completely and give him a normal work schedule so he could spend nights at home.

I started 5th grade at Shasta Elementary School. No longer on a military base, I was the new kid in the class. It was a culture shock, and I was teased for my short height, mile-long bangs, super thick glasses, and being cold all the time.

As I grew older, the teasing got worse, but I ignored it. Boys asked me out as a ploy to be mean, but I never fell for it. Why would I want to give them the time of the day? To get me involved, my dad put me in the softball league. I enjoyed being part of the team and didn't mind playing in the outfield.

COMMANDER TO CROWN

One day I was practicing with the coach's son. He hit a pop fly. I caught it with my glove—which was from my dad and was over 30 years old—but it broke. Luckily, I was wearing my glasses, and they took the brunt of the force of the ball breaking through the glove and hitting my face. It left me with a black eye and ring cut on my cheek from the frames that broke.

The next day was picture day for our team, and my parents wouldn't let me sit it out. I couldn't wear glasses because of the injury, so I went to school without them. Since I was farsighted, I felt I could see fine—until my mom took me to the eye doctor a few days later. Without my glasses, I felt like a new person at school. It's scary to think how an object on our face can change how we perceive and experience the world. This new confidence made me want contacts permanently, but I knew that would take a lot of patience and convincing of my parents.

I persevered, and I entered middle school that year with contacts and a perm, the popular hair trend in the 90's. I felt like a new person, and my confidence renewed. Nevertheless, middle school was tough. I saw kids who started to drink alcohol, join gangs and do things I knew would be destructive. I also saw kids date, hold hands, and kiss in the hallways. One kid, Chris Clayton, had a crush on me, but being raised in a military household, I wasn't allowed to have boyfriends, especially in the 7th grade.

Tired of trying to fit in, I hoped high school would be better. Since we hadn't moved in four years, I thought we were staying put, so I tried out for the Manteca High School Cheerleading squad. There were 50 of us for 12 spots. I had zero cheerleading experience, but for the first time, my petite stature helped. I could be a flyer. Sadly, I made the team only to find out we were moving again—this time to Reno, Nevada.

I was devastated. It took me four years to finally feel accepted by others and feel like I belonged—only to move again. I had no choice but to start over again.

Life is beautiful, messy, and never goes according to plan.

My dad officially retired during a beautiful ceremony on the USS Mercy and decided it was time for the family to put down some roots. My father was from Connecticut in New England and loved the mountains. My mother, a true Southern Californian, who loved her sunshine and ocean, agreed to the Lake Tahoe and Nevada area because it was close to her family. Plus, we could afford a bigger house than in California. So, my dad bought a private practice, and Reno was our new home.

We moved in just three days before I started at Galena High School. It was tough to enter a high school where everyone knew each other, and I knew no one. They all had gone to elementary school and middle school together, and I was the new kid again. It was also hard to feel like I belonged, because many of the girls idolized the seniors and weren't interested in talking to a newbie like me.

During my first two years, I was on the tennis team and focused on doing well in school. I got good grades but still wanted to feel more like I belonged. I was smaller, underdeveloped, and hadn't hit puberty yet, so I felt like a 12-year-old boy with long hair.

Before my junior year, I took a leap of faith and tried out for the cheerleading team. To my surprise, I made it, and I swapped my tennis skirt out for a cheerleading skirt. I got a lot of grief for switching sports, but I knew I needed the change—both of sports and who I was surrounded by.

My experience in high school drastically changed. I had met a group of women who valued their academics as much as their relationships. I saw that the measure of friendship is not how you feel about someone else but how they make you feel about yourself.

During my senior year, I became a parliamentarian in the student council. Although I didn't feel popular, I felt like people knew who I was and respected me. I remember even getting my little brother to be selected to participate in a rally his freshman year. Nick was mortified and told me later he was embarrassed. I was shocked and thought I was helping him get popular and well-known in school since I didn't know anyone when I started there.

I was happy to earn a 3.9 GPA and graduate with honors to finish school. I felt on top of the world and grateful to start at St. Mary's College that Fall.

(March 1991: Our first family photo after my father arrived home from deployment with Operation Desert Storm)

Advice

Often when we don't get our way or things don't go according to our plans, it's not until later we realize that God had other ideas for us. However, to be open to better things moving forward we have to look past what we think is best.

Nothing changes if you don't change. To change your life, you must change your environment, change who you associate with, and often take a leap of faith to change the world around you.

This leap was often forced upon me because of my military upbringing. Life is a game. Find the games you want to play, learn the rules, and find a way to be successful. These were all lessons I learned growing up. No matter what label is put on you, only you can define yourself.

CHAPTER 2: COLLEGE

Timeline
Chapter 2

1999
Began my freshman year at St. Mary's College of California as a Health Science major and lived in an all-female dormitory.

2000
During summer break, I worked at my dad's dental office and spent my free time with girlfriends from high school.

Began my sophomore year in the Fall.

2001
During summer break, I helped my dad in a mobile dental van and met a young girl who changed the trajectory of my life.

At the start of my Junior year, Mrs. Johnson told me not to go to dental school but get a "Mrs. degree" instead.

Switched my major to Communications with a Science minor.

After an awkward PR experience with the basketball team, I joined the rowing team as a coxswain.

2002
During summer break, I volunteered at health fairs and worked for a few other dentists, including a pediatric dentist.

At the beginning of my senior year, I enacted a new plan to improve my grades to get into dental school.

2003
Graduated from college.

Freshman Year

Back in California for my first semester at St. Mary's College, I resided in Assumption, an all-female dorm. There were lots of jokes made about this dorm by other college kids. A common crass saying was, "If you want to get some action, go to 'the ass on the 2nd floor.'" It was easy for boys to get a lot of female attention there.

My first roommate Jenny was from Hawaii and was truly a fish out of the water. Initially, I felt bad she didn't feel like she belonged and helped her when I could. We were both from out of state and didn't know anyone when we arrived. I was gone most of the day at the library studying or cheerleading practice before cheering at the games at night.

Whenever I came home, Jenny was either sleeping or wanting to go out. I had a heavy academic workload, so this was hard on me.

Our relationship began to unravel when I started noticing my clothes were not where I put them. I later discovered she had borrowed my things without asking. When I confronted her, she said she wouldn't do it again but did. I remember being at a party and seeing her wearing a red top that I had thrown in my hamper to wash.

I majored in Health Science and wanted to go to medical school, and she wasn't sure what she wanted to major in. I was committed to big goals, and she was still half-heartedly searching. So it was hard for us to connect and build a real friendship.

Then one night I came home late from the library and found Jenny making out with a guy on my bed for the second time that week. She brushed me off and just complained that the bunk beds we had were inconvenient—hers was the top bunk. I was really pissed off. It was then I knew this situation had to change and luckily found there was another set of roommates in the dorm hall who were asking for a swap as well.

My new roommate Jen and I instantly bonded over our love for makeup, fashion, and all things sunny in California. Although our fields of study were very different, we had mutual respect. I was grateful that we got along and always shared our space well. Imagine an 8-foot by 10-foot room with two twin beds, two desks, and two closets. Space was tight.

When I wasn't in class or at cheer practice, I spent every hour I could in the library, focused on my studies. I figured I would just "get it." But even after re-reading and re-reviewing the science materials over and over, I didn't. My Health Science classes were tough.

One brother who taught my General Chemistry class infamously claimed, "Not even God gets an A in my class." He was right. Of the 60 people in our class, only ten finished. I got a C. It was my first ever, and my heart sank.

How was I going to tell my parents?

Here I was going to a ridiculously expensive private school in the San Francisco bay area. I lived in the dorms, had no car, had no cell phone, ate at the cafeteria, yet all the scholarships I received were spent after my 1st semester. I knew I needed to do better. I knew I could do better.

My only escapes from the rigors of school were cheerleading and the occasional girls' night out at a dance club in the city. One club we liked went by a different name depending on the night and was the only one that let in 18-year-olds. The promoters gave me a VIP card because they said my "look" would bring in more business. I was a skinny, blue-eyed blonde who had also inherited her mother's ample butt. As a VIP, I skipped the line, paid no cover charge, and felt special.

Freshman Year's Summer Break

That summer, my parents had me go to my dad's office back home to help him so I could save money for college expenses while taking summer school. I knew that if I wanted to have better grades and a better life, I needed to do what others wouldn't do.

What made summer especially fun was that three other blondes I became close to in high school—Randy, Greta, and Melissa—were back home too. We would go on road trips to Tahoe, cruise downtown, attend college fraternity parties together, and check out festivals. What's more, we looked out for each other.

Every time summer ended, the reality of our having to go our separate ways set in. I'd head back to college in California, and they went back to school in Nevada. During the summer, our friendship strengthened, but while in school, we were just not as connected via the phone.

The high stakes of academics and pressure to succeed kept me busy. Plus, every time my dad drove me back in his large white pickup truck loaded with all my belongings, he reminded me of the sacrifices he and my mom were making.

Sophomore Year

During my sophomore year, I lived in a suite with my friend Heather and another girl named Anna. It was a 2-bedroom that shared a bathroom with another 2-bedroom. That year I was with Heather 24/7. We lived together, cheered together, and went out together. During Freshman year, we had lived in the same dorm and talked about how we would be perfect roommates.

Unfortunately, after just one semester, I realized we spent too much time together. However, I was scared to hurt her feelings, so I put her needs ahead of mine. I was a people-pleaser. I cared about her feelings more than my own. For example, at cheer some of the girls didn't care for her and wanted to put her in the back of the routine. I would take her spot because I wanted her to be happy and for everyone to like me.

Sacrificing my needs for hers took a toll on me mentally, and I wasn't sleeping well. I knew it would hurt our friendship to speak up, but sometimes the hardest things to do are really for the best. She had started dating—and ended up marrying—a guy in the military in secret. So the dynamics of our friendship and living situation were changing dramatically anyhow.

I was beginning to understand how important it was to voice my needs and be true to myself. Being a people-pleaser is exhausting, and if you are not being authentic, it will take a toll, chipping away inside of you over time. I made sure the roommate change was in place for Junior year.

Sophomore Year's Summer Break

Summer break, back home after my sophomore year, changed the trajectory of my life. I assisted my dad in a mobile dental van in providing free dental care and exams to 2nd graders in schools located in impoverished areas of Reno, Nevada.

I met an eight-year-old girl who would change my life. I can remember it like it was yesterday. Karen walked in scared, anxious, and nervous. When she sat down and opened her mouth, my dad motioned me to look. There were holes, places where her permanent teeth should be, that had rotted down to the bone. I was heartbroken.

How was this possible in Reno? I wasn't in a third-world war-torn country. I was in my hometown. This innocent child had to take an aspirin every night for the pain because her parents couldn't afford to take her to the dentist.

How could this be? She should be able to laugh, play, and eat all the foods kids love. Not this. It was then that I realized I wanted to be a voice for her and knew my career and goals had to change. To be that voice and speak for her, I needed to go to dental school to have credentials and leverage to make an impact.

Junior Year

When I arrived back at school, I made an appointment to speak with my career counselor Mrs. Johnson. I marched into her office with determination and declared my new goal.

She put down her coffee, looked me up and down, and said, "You are never going to get in. You are dreaming. No one in our college has gotten into dental school in the last four years. Your grades are subpar, and your extracurriculars are unimpressive. What makes you think you can do it?"

I was stunned. But she wasn't done.

"Your goals are ridiculous; they are completely unreachable. You should be focusing on getting married—get a 'Mrs. Degree' instead," Mrs. Johnson added.

She was right, I thought to myself. Maybe I do aim too high. Maybe I'm not good enough to walk in my father's footsteps. I left her office dejected.

However, as I made my way back to my dorm, I started to get angry. The angrier I got, the more I realized she was wrong.

Am I going to let someone else dictate my future?

Am I going to let someone who doesn't know me well tell me my limits and what is or isn't possible for my life?

No, I am not. No, I will not.

My life and path are up to me. I get to decide. This is my future. I have to remember my motivation: that 8-year-old girl and all the kids who need my help.

So, instead of going the traditional route (or focusing on catching myself a husband), I changed my major to Communications with a Science minor so that I could graduate in four years. After the switch, I was happier than ever before. I really understood the courses and especially enjoyed Public Relations.

I began to network with alumni and game attendees when I cheered. I figured before I went to dental school I would work for dental companies and be a speaker utilizing my growing communications skills. My first internship involved providing public relations to the women's basketball team who had gone to the NCAA tournament the previous few years. I was excited to have this opportunity to get real-world experience for a group of women who I admired and were proud to support.

But then my world shook when I had to defend our women's basketball team when their star player was caught cheating on one of her exams. I felt like I was walking on a balance beam of truth and reputation. I knew public relations for this team was critical moving forward, so I had to put a positive spin on it and talk around the truth. I didn't like it. I began to feel that people only talked to me because of my appearance and not for the intellect or skill I brought to the table. I realized that this was detracting from my dream of eventually being a dentist and that I needed to go all in, now.

That night when I got back to the dorm, I shared what happened with my roommate Brianna who was very kind and a great listener. She reminded me of a soon-to-be soccer mom. She had an adorable boyfriend, and despite our differences in goals, our morals and values gave us a strong connection. I shared who I had crushes on, and she always knew what to say even when I had a rough day.

That year, I was approached by my friends Dario and Ryan in my townhouse building to join the men's varsity rowing team. They needed a small, petite, light-weight person who could be loud, motivating, and competitive. They convinced me that I was perfect for their team.

So, I joined without realizing this meant freezing mornings on the water starting at 5 am to yell and motivate a crew. You're probably thinking why? They were in need of coxswains who sat at the front or rear of the boat to motivate and drive the boat. Usually, the coxswain is usually a light-weight person because he or she is dead weight since they are not rowing. At first, I wasn't sure if I had the time to do it, since I hadn't had a free summer break to relax but something kept telling me these guys would teach me discipline and leadership in being part of their team.

I had no clue what I was doing at first, but the guys treated me well. I was their little sister. We all worked well together and built up a great rapport. As a coxswain, I wore a CoxBox, a headset with a microphone that projected my voice over the entire boat and out to neighboring boats too. One morning I figured out how to play Dave Matthews on a CD player that I connected to the microphone and used this when I knew they needed an extra push from a late night out. We meshed so well that they welcomed my help to recruit a few more petite females to become coxswains, too.

Every rowing race is known as a regatta. And the tradition is to throw the coxswain into the water, which happened to me – with all my clothes on – after every race. About halfway through the season I was able to convince my crew that before throwing in to have mercy and allow me to take my shoes off since the lake water destroyed them.

The crystal glass water in the morning that we pierced with our oars gave me a sense of calm and peace. I spoke over my Coxbox to motivate the crew, and the leader in front of me, known as the Stroke, assisted me every time we rowed by setting the pace with the boat. After row practice I would rush home to shower, go to class, study, and then zoom to cheer practice. Throw in the occasional student council meeting and one can see I didn't have a lot of down time to relax. But having purpose in a lot of pursuits made me focused.

The men on this team allowed me to take a set of skills I learned in cheerleading and channel in another way-leadership, never accepting that there is one road to success and there's much more to the sport than winning.

Never underestimate the talents that you are born with whether it's in sports, academics, street smarts, resilience you name it. If you choose to use them, work on them and grow with them you will never realize the full potential of what you are capable of. These men taught me you don't stop when you are tired, you stop when you are done. You must stay in beast mode, as they called it.

What do you do on days when you don't feel like crushing it? Those are the days that define your life.

By switching my major and trying new things, I opened myself up to new worlds. That year I also met Jennifer Benjamin, a business major who lived at the library like I did. We worked on project after project together and a deep friendship grew out from the tall lines of books that surrounded us each day (18 years later our friendship is still growing strong, as we each pave the way as leaders in our respective industries).

Junior Year's Summer Break

On the annual drive home with my dad, he began to ask me what I wanted to do. I wasn't completely sure yet because I loved working at his office, but I was a horrible dental assistant. One time I spilled bleach on a patient's black sweater. Oh, how I cringed because I knew I would be paying for it both at work with a salary cut and at home with extra chores.

I decided to volunteer at health fairs to learn more too. My dad always stressed the importance of giving back; it was a value he wanted to instill in my brother and me. So, volunteering felt great, and it helped me see what other potential paths there were for me. I didn't have to be just a general dentist but could also work for the American Dental Association, Give Kids A Smile nonprofit, be a consultant for dental companies, go into sales, marketing—you name it.

Then, my dad suggested I work with a few other dentists to see if I would like that area, too. I worked with Dr. Trujillo, a pediatric dentist, and loved it. The kids were hilarious, and I loved the fast-paced energy of the place. It was like the cement wasn't dry—kids were capable of change and far more open to it than adults. By contrast, my dad's long procedures were a bit dull, but the idea I could bounce from one procedure to the next with back-to-back appointments worked for me. I liked developing relationships with my patients through good communication with them, their siblings, and their parents.

From the volunteer health fairs, helping in my dad's practice, and working in the pediatric dentistry office, I felt like I tried a lot of things and finally knew that working with kids was where I wanted to go and serve. I also wanted to speak at dental conferences.

Now all I had to do was get into dental school! I didn't have the grades in the required nine (courses that dental and medical schools scrutinized) to get in. My C's in general chemistry were not going to be waived by my A's in communications courses. So, I began to search with whom I could take classes and also looked to retake the required courses in which I received less than a B+. I found UC Berkeley offered Biochemistry online, and Kaplan offered a Dental Admissions Test (DAT) preparatory course. My local universities offered the Chemistry and Biology classes I needed to retake.

A plan was formed, and now I had to execute it.

Senior Year

Because I knew dental schools were hungry for students who were not only smart but also compassionate, in my senior year, I focused hard on my dissertation—a unique requirement of my Communications major.

So, with clarity and renewed energy, I completed my final year in college with a laser focus on getting into dental school.

(Left to right: Archie Gomez, Casey Nelson, me, and Quinn Draper at UNLV graduation)

Advice

The experience in the counselor's office taught me that sometimes you can't put all your trust in one person to determine your future, especially when they have already made up their mind about you. I've learned in my journey that before you can help people in life who come to you for advice, skills, talent, or mentorship, you need to gain their trust and learn how to communicate with them.

Some people are visual learners, others are auditory, spatial, logistical, or social, and this often determines how you, the person helping them, communicates. My communications major in college opened my eyes to how to do this; I learned how to make people feel less anxious and more comfortable inside a dental office. It is very important to me.

"You can't go back and change the beginning, but you can start where you are and change the ending." —C.S Lewis

You can't stop being who you are because you are afraid. When you know what you want, you go after it with certainty that you will find a way to make it happen. This blind faith and trust are the keys to making your goals a reality. When there is no clear road to follow, simply leave a trail.

Despite the bumps (getting my first C), brick walls (my college counselor), and naysayers who didn't think I could, I constantly faced along my journey and knew there were obstacles for a reason: to show me how badly I wanted it.

Engage in relationships in the way you want them to look for you. You can't control other people's actions, but you can control yours and how you react to theirs. Spend time only with friends who believe in you, who speak about the future, and make you excited to see them. Surround yourself with energy-givers, people who add value to your life.

Sometimes the best moments in your life are also the most humbling ones. Getting my first C in college and having to retake the science courses that dental schools wanted to see As in were mine.

Have daily goals, life goals, and yearly goals. Understand that to achieve your goals you must apply discipline and consistency. You must work at them every day with a plan that you enact.

If you can dream it, you can do it. This motto inspires me to keep pursuing my dream to change the doctor-patient relationship in my industry by building trust and encouraging deep, open-ended, and vulnerable conversation.

CHAPTER 3:
DENTAL SCHOOL

Timeline
Chapter 3

2002 During the fall of my Senior year, I applied to 10 dental schools with my special 120-page Communications thesis and got put on the waitlist for two of them.

2003 In April, I was accepted into the dental school at UNLV and took my oath as an Ensign as a Navy HPSP student.

In the summer, I moved to Las Vegas.

In the fall, I began dental school as one of only 18 women in a class of 75 students.

2005 In the third year of dental school, we relocated downtown to work in the clinic.

I was told I had a personality for orthodontics (and fell in love with it while working with Dr. T).

2007 To finish my senior year of dental school, I recruited patients from local women's shelters to give free dental care while earning experience to pass my board requirements.

On May 11, I graduated as a dentist.

On May 12, I took my oath as a Lieutenant in the Navy.

During the fall of my senior year, I applied to 10 dental schools and interviewed at Creighton University in Omaha, Nebraska and the University of Nevada, Las Vegas. Both put me on the waitlist.

My chances to get in were slim, but I hoped my Communications thesis would set me apart. Entitled *Tell-Show-Do: Effective Communication Strategies Dentists Use for Children in Public Healthcare,* it worked in my passions for both dentistry and public healthcare. It was my answer to why I wanted to go to dental school.

From my summer breaks at health fairs and mobile dental vans, I was interviewed and gathered the information needed to complete my dissertation in record time. I learned that first impressions in the doctor-patient relationship set the foundation for future visits, treatment, and education. This unique relationship is built on trust, respect, communication, and a common understanding on both sides.

From pediatric dentists to general dentists to assistants and those in public healthcare, I began to see the numerous challenges today's dentistry faces with impoverished populations and those who make just enough above what's considered poverty, preventing them from qualifying for needed government assistance.

This 120-page thesis is what I proudly carried to each of the dental school interviews that I had in the winter of my senior year in college. In addition to only A's in nine required courses, high DAT Scores, and letters of recommendation from dentists, dental schools also looked for students with majors in Biology, Zoology, and Chemistry. I opted for a path that was unconventional with a major in Communications.

It was a bit of a gamble, but I had to be true to my passions. Plus, I also knew these schools wanted something more than someone who was just book smart and looked good on paper. They also wanted candidates who could handle the challenges of what a dentist is in today's society. My thesis helped me demonstrate that I was ready and committed.

But how was I going to pay for it? I had just finished four years at a private catholic college in the San Francisco bay area, so there was no way my parents could afford another four years. I looked up what the military offered and found the Health Professions Scholarship Program (HPSP). It would pay for your dental school 100% and give a stipend, too.

How hard could it be to be accepted to the HPSP? Well, I met with a recruiter, flew down to San Diego, and was whisked away to another world. I walked into the naval base known as "32nd Street" and saw everyone in scrubs, talking with each other on a friendly first-name basis. Everyone was confident and cool.

Is this what life in the Navy would be? I could handle this.

The idea of serving my country, taking care of those who defended our freedom, and focusing on school —not the cost of my education—was a win-win situation for me. So, I applied for both the Navy and the Air Force HPSP programs and included great letters of recommendation from connections in the military I had met through my father. It turned out that coming from a military family really helped. Getting selected for the HPSP was more competitive than I realized.

Luckily, I got word from the Navy HPSP that they would accept me if I got into dental school. I was excited at the prospect of continuing the legacy of military service like my father (a retired naval officer and dentist), my mother (former civil servant for the Navy), and my little brother (a reserve submarine petty officer at the time).

On April 1, 2003, I was in my senior year at St. Mary's college and heard my phone ring. When I answered, a man named Mr. Davenport said, "I'm pleased to offer you a spot at UNLV Class of 2007."

Before he even finished his sentence, I practically shouted, "Yes! When do I start?!" as I jumped on top of my bed and screamed with joy at the top of my lungs.

I did it! I got in!

I was the first person from my college in four years to get into dental school.

The teachers who told me I wouldn't survive Calculus or pass Chemistry, the career counselor who told me I had no chance of getting in—they were all wrong. I was going to UNLV to become a dentist.

After forwarding the news to the Navy recruiter, I took my oath of office as an Ensign and officially became a Navy HPSP student. Not only did I figure out a way to get into dental school, but I also managed to get it paid for and ensure I'd have a job upon graduation.

Over the summer, I moved to Las Vegas to get settled in. My parents bought a home in the Southern Highlands area and wanted to teach me how to be a landlord while completing dental school. It was overwhelming, to say the least. I went from sharing a three-bedroom, one-bath townhouse to overseeing a four-bedroom, two-and-a-half-bath house. In many ways, it was a dream come true to have my own bedroom and bathroom for the first time in my life. My parents made me the onsite property manager, and it became my responsibility to find roommates. I was lucky enough to have wonderful neighbors across the street who helped me manage repairs around the house since my parents lived six hours away.

Despite having a Navy scholarship to alleviate financial concerns, dental school was tough. It was a lot harder than college. In my first month of dental school, I was stressed to the max, taking one test after the next. Every week I felt like I was taking finals.

I got up early and stayed up late to study at the library as much as possible. Every day after class, my classmates and I would get a Jamba Juice and then hide in our respective corners in the library to escape from the world and focus on the material that would be tested on the following day.

Although I always felt confident answering questions in the class, I'd feel the panic rise with a test in front of me. For each question, I'd say an answer in my head but then look at the scantron and change my answer at the last minute. I kept doubting myself. I did this overthinking freak out for every question and, ultimately, I failed the test. This happened again and again. Even though I knew the answer, I second-guessed myself and changed the answer for every single question.

As a result, I failed all my exams in every class during my first month in dental school. I was on the verge of losing my Navy scholarship and my dream of becoming a dentist.

Then, one of my teachers pulled me aside and said, "Corinne, I know you know this material. Let's do an oral exam."

During classes and at review sessions, I had always raised my hand to answer her questions. I was always an active, participatory, and dedicated student. Dr. Galbraith could see that. So she had been surprised at the low test scores.

"I'm not ready, Dr. Galbraith," I replied crestfallen. "I haven't prepared for an oral exam, and I don't want to let you down even more."

"No, you are ready. I know you know the material," Dr. Galbraith replied before proceeding to ask me one question after the next.

I answered each question as best I could. At the end of the session, Dr. Galbraith looked down at her notes and up at me.

"You got an A."

"What?!"

"I will replace the D you got on my previous exam with an A," she said smiling.

I could feel a light shine through a window into my soul. That moment changed everything for me. Someone truly believed in me, and I went and requested to test that way with most of my other professors. I was incredibly grateful for their kindness and patience with me since this was not typical.

Thanks to Dr. Galbraith, I learned how to work through test anxiety and discovered a new way to conquer the exams. From that moment on, I looked at my failures as opportunities to learn. My relationship with failure changed from a sense of desperation to celebration. We all have that opportunity to learn and grow.

All of my teachers—many of whom had military affiliations—really impressed me with how well-rounded and innovative they were. Those with military experience often reflected on their time serving. For example, Dr. Louise Saunders and her husband Dr. Michael Saunders served in the Army National Guard and did reserve time as dentists before committing to dental education full time. Dr. Richards had enlisted in the service before becoming a dentist. I aspired to develop a similar balance of multiple passions.

In my class of 75 students, there were only 18 women. I made friends with Lisa, Carolina, and Deedee. We all bonded over our love of chocolate and the camaraderie of being in the minority—by gender and lifestyle—in our class. We believed in working hard and playing hard, whereas most other students (many who were Mormon) saw going to any party as inappropriate. After our first round of tests, we went out on the town, got bottle service using our local connection, and toasted to completing the first of many academic hurdles.

As dental school progressed, so did the stress, but the environment changed. During our third year, we relocated downtown to work in the clinic—patients were now our homework. We no longer had the university campus with endless libraries at our fingertips or a Jamba Juice stand a short five-minute walk away. Outside the doorsteps of our dental school downtown, we encountered homeless people, drug addicts, and ladies of the night. Our places to study became scarce and quiet spaces were challenging to find.

I knew that to continue my dream to help the 8-year-old who changed my life, I needed to take additional post-graduate training after completing dental school. And to get into a pediatric residency program, I needed to work with pediatric dentists under multiple internships. So I went to the University of Florida, the

University of California in Los Angeles, and Indiana University each for one-week programs.

During these programs, I observed how dentists are an integral part of their patients' lives. It was hard to see small children have repeat visits to the operating room, taking an enormous time, energy, and financial toll on the family. I gasped when I met several children who battled cerebral palsy so severe that they had to be fed through a gastrointestinal tube connected to their belly button. Seeing suffering in such young, innocent kids made me question if this was the right profession for me after all.

Back in dental school in Las Vegas, we had all walks of life come through our doors who truly loved having students work on them. I remember one of my classmates, Carolina, had patients who dressed up like Elvis, Captain Jack Sparrow from the Pirates of the Caribbean, and other famous characters. Some of these people were entertainers on the Las Vegas Strip, others put on a show for us dental students just for fun. It made our day and reminded us of the impact we were making in the community.

During my third year, Dr. Brownstein, the Dean of Student Affairs, suggested I work with a local pediatric dentist in Las Vegas named Dr. Waggoner. Dr. Brownstein knew I wanted to be a pediatric dentist and that I had a deep admiration for Dr. Waggoner. He had taught at Iowa University Pediatric Program before going into private practice. His office was beautiful and ran with a well-orchestrated flow of patients, parents, and assistants.

One day, Dr. Waggoner asked me to distract the orthodontist Dr. Carl T. Loeffler (aka Dr. T) because they wanted to surprise him for his birthday. While talking with him, he said he had watched me in the clinic and thought I had the personality of an orthodontist. I told him I didn't know what that meant.

"Just come work with me to try it out. I'll smooth things out with Dr. Waggoner," he replied.

I never had braces, so I had no experience as a patient, and the students I knew who wanted to be orthodontists were "the gunners," as we called them. They would do literally anything to earn an A, so I didn't feel like I fit into their crowd. But I figured I had nothing to lose.

It's great that I was open to it because I fell in love with orthodontics. Dr. T even took his American Board of Orthodontics certificate off the wall, made a copy, wrote my name over his name, and handed me a copy (he also kept one for himself). The power of having someone believe in you is so powerful. Plus, this simple visual representation helped plant the seed in my subconscious that it was truly possible.

During my senior year in dental school, my classmates and I realized we needed to find patients who had the perfect cavity (one seen clear as day on an x-ray in the shape of a triangle pointing to the center of the pulp of a tooth) and calculus (appearing as spikes sticking out like thorns on a rose-marked with pride on bitewing x-rays). Cavities and calculus were our prized "board patients," a requirement for the clinical portion to be allowed to practice dentistry after graduating from dental school. I had no idea how I would do this since the cost to get patients from dental companies could be outrageous. So, I began to think about patients who needed dental care but couldn't afford it.

The previous year we participated in Give Kids a Smile Day and also Smiles for Success where we took care of women who came from a local shelter. So, we reached out to those incredible organizations. With a little bit of convincing and coordination of rides, food, and daycare, these women were able to get free dental care and help two of my fellow female dentists and me to pass our boards. The courage these women showed was our inspiration.

Two months later, I graduated. And on the day following our formal graduation, on May 12, 2007, I left a pool party at the Mirage to take my oath as a Lieutenant in the U.S. Navy. My classmates wore their Sunday-best collared shirts and ties since they had just come from church. I wore my bikini.

Was I out of place? Yes.

Not only was I the only female, but I was also determined to bring who I was to the Navy. All of me.

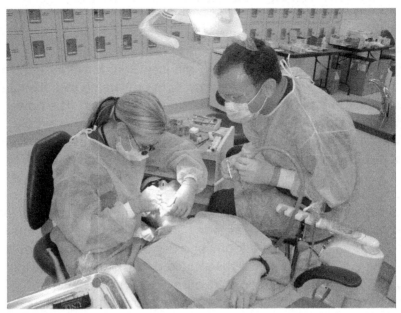

(A fellow dental school colleague and me, providing free dental care with Smiles for Success for a female patient)

Advice

When you need help, don't be afraid to ask for it and keep asking until you get the support you need.

When you help and serve others, the acts of kindness will fill you up more than receiving anything yourself.

Focus on progress, not perfection. Did I learn something? Did I move one more inch closer towards my goal? Stick with it even if there are setbacks. If it's worth it to you, you will find a way.

Progress equals happiness. Working toward progress, big or small, gives you a reason to be alive. We all need to grow and feel like we are transforming for the better.

"Yesterday is history, tomorrow is a mystery, but today is a gift. That's why we call it 'the present.'" —Eleanor Roosevelt.

The only person you are destined to become is the person you decide to be. We have three choices in life: give up, give in, or give it everything you've got.

Along the way, I developed mental toughness, which is different from motivation. Where mental toughness kicks in on the days when it's dark, cold, and you don't want to get out of bed although you know you have to.

Success happens outside your comfort zone. You must train your brain by consistently doing things that make you uncomfortable. You have to build the mindset that when things get hard, you don't shy away, you don't quit—you forge on.

See through all the walls and focus on where you want to go. Don't just climb that mountain, enjoy climbing that mountain.

CHAPTER 4: PAGEANTS

Timeline
Chapter 4

2005

During my 2nd year of dental school, a classmate dared me to enter a pageant and do better than second runner-up.

In the fall, I entered my first pageant for the Miss Nevada USA crown and earned first runner-up.

2006

I worked hard to improve.

2007

In May, I graduated from dental school, took my oath with the Navy, and won Ms. Nevada 2007.

In June, I began work in the Navy.

In July, I competed in the national pageant and placed in the top five.

2008

I competed in the Miss International system in Chicago but didn't place.

I took a step back to compete in smaller systems to hone my skills and hired a pageant coach.

At the end of the year, I won Miss All American 2009.

2009 - 2021

Since 2009, all while being deployed overseas as a naval officer, I have been blessed to win:

Ms. United America 2009
Ms. Texas United States 2012
Ms. United States 2012
Ms. Galaxy 2014
Ms. Earth 2018
International Ms. 2020

Have you ever dared to do something completely out of your comfort zone and against every instinct of your being but did it anyway, and it changed your life?

In 2005, while in my second year of dental school, one of my classmates started telling me about what she had watched on TV the night before.

"I caught the end of the Miss USA pageant," Lisa said. "And the girl who was second runner-up is a dental student at the University of North Carolina."

"Oh?" I replied nonchalantly.

"Yeah," Lisa continued, "It made me think of you. Have you ever thought of entering a pageant?"

Before I could answer, another classmate behind us laughed and said, "Oh, Corinne could never do that!"

I turned around and gave him a darting look. I couldn't believe he had been eavesdropping on our conversation.

"I dare you to do better," he taunted.

"You know what? Watch me!" I snapped back.

That fall, I entered the Miss Nevada USA pageant. When I walked into orientation, I was suddenly surrounded by women who had competed in pageants since they were little girls, and here I was at 24 years old and only doing my first one.

I felt like a fish out of water.

I was not prepared for what it would feel like to be judged on a stage by strangers standing under bright lights in just a swimsuit or glimmering evening gown. I had no idea what a pageant interview was, let alone experience answering tough questions like, "What is the one most important thing that our society needs?"

Everyone knows the answer to that one is world peace. But how do you say it in an elegant, concise way under pressure?

This was way outside my comfort zone.

I had a strong personality and a huge drive for academic, physical, and professional success. But aren't pageant girls just about wearing pretty clothes, smiling for cameras, and pointlessly perfecting the pageant wave?

I used to think pageants were shallow and only for girls who wanted to parade around with crowns on their heads. I didn't get the point or understand why they did them in the first place.

However, I soon learned it was about so much more. I entered a world full of women who were driven, ambitious, and beautiful both inside and out. I immediately felt a sense of camaraderie similar to what I experienced in the military.

I found that the competition and the stage gave me a place to push, improve, and fully express myself. The beauty of life is that you can always change, grow, and get better. You aren't defined by your past or your mistakes.

My preconceived notions about pageant girls and women had been all wrong. Self-improvement, self-care, self-esteem, generosity, healthy living, physical fitness, ambition, and worldliness were just a few qualities they all held dear.

Despite my lack of experience and initial biases, I proudly earned first runner-up. And I was hooked. Only one person can walk away with the crown, but I walked away with friends who made me feel amazing about who I was even at moments when I was feeling weak and not enough.

In terms of self-improvement, one mistake that I realized I made while competing was with my pageant walk across the stage. After my first competition, I watched the video of the entire event and realized that when I got excited, my arms swung, and my head bobbled. It was incredibly distracting.

After getting support from a local modeling agency, they had me start walking on a balance beam only six inches wide and raised off the floor to gain control over my walk. With practice, I improved a lot. It also helped to remind myself to stay calm, take a deep breath, and just enjoy the moment.

I have learned so much by competing in pageants far beyond walking with poise and confidence. I also learned how to enter a world where I could be strong, feminine, and confidently vulnerable while simultaneously being subjectively judged by others on a stage. This didn't come naturally at first.

At the Miss International pageant, for example, there were 87 delegates from all over the world. I met women on the path to becoming doctors, lawyers, social workers, entrepreneurs, and more. They each worked to advance a cause and charity near to their hearts. I didn't place in the top 15, but it taught me what I got right and in what areas I needed to improve.

For example, my strengths were maintaining my physical shape, being mentally balanced, and maintaining my energy. On the other hand, I needed to improve my interviewing by fine-tuning my answer delivery and learning how to lead the interview with confidence. I also need to work on my wardrobe and moving in new gowns in a graceful way that also made me look and feel much taller.

I watched and admired women around me who weren't the typical body shape seen winning on TV—taller than 5'7", size 2, and a mere 100 to 110 pounds—but they graced the stage as if they owned it nonetheless.

The winner that year was only 5'5", deaf, and what you might imagine a Crossfit competition champion. Her heart and spirit were pure gold, and we rushed to her after she was crowned on stage to shower her with congratulations. Pageants have taught me that we are all built differently, and there are many ways to feel beautiful.

What is a beauty queen? Poised, present, and polished. She knows true beauty comes from within—a fact that people can't help but notice when they get to know her. No matter the environment she is in or whom she is with, she carries herself with grace and strives to make herself and the world better.

My pageant journey continued in Nevada for a couple of years until I won Ms. Nevada 2007 in the United States system. The timing was remarkable because I won in May, just one week after graduating from dental school and taking my oath with the Navy.

Then, on June 26, 2007, I reported for duty. I felt so honored to have won a title but was also very nervous because there I was, a brand new officer, walking into my boss's office on my first day in the Navy to ask a question I was sure would be denied.

"Sir, can I take one week of leave right away to go back to Las Vegas to compete in the national pageant?" I asked nervously.

"Yes," replied Commander Joseph Molinaro, the Residency Director of the Advanced Education in General Dentistry, without hesitation.

I couldn't believe it! I was able to make it work before residency had me in rotations. I placed in the top five that July and knew I wanted to compete more. Pageantry had given me more confidence, elevated my public speaking skills, improved my posture, and forced me to own who I was.

Commander Molinaro later shared with me how he could see that competing helped me become a more engaged naval officer. He told me about a female officer he had worked with who had won Miss Maryland before entering the Navy. He said he was always in awe of her poise, manners, and decorum from speaking to crowds and one-on-one interaction. He wanted me to have the same opportunity to grow my skills in those areas. I'm indebted to his foresight and grace.

The following year in 2008, I competed in the Miss International system in Chicago. There were 87 women; it was my biggest pageant yet, and the pressure was on. I had never been in a competition where everyone was photoshoot-ready at all times with the perfect hair, professional makeup, and couture outfits. The other women changed their clothes several times a day. I literally ran out of outfits and was grateful to Miss South Carolina and Miss North Carolina for letting me borrow their sparkly tops.

I didn't place or win, but I made a great group of friends who taught me that you have to be yourself and let the judges see you as authentic and confident when you walk into an interview, which is the first part of the competition and takes place a few days before the stage components. The day I did my interview, I ran back to my hotel room and threw myself on my bed, overanalyzing every answer I gave. Stressing about my performance plagued me over the next few days too.

Luckily, my pageant friends reminded me that you can't compare yourself to anyone else and have to be the best version of yourself that you can be. This advice was terrific, but I found it easier said than done. Some girls had entire teams of hair and makeup artists, coaches, and directors plus wardrobe options to last them for three weeks. The girls from Great Britain and Poland, by contrast, could only bring two checked bags' worth of clothes. But, they reasoned, anyone who needed a pile of clothes, lots of makeup, and expensive hair products to show who they really were was only masking their true selves.

After this competition, I decided to take a step back and compete in a smaller national system to better understand what I needed to succeed in big-stage pageantry. So I entered the All American Miss system and hired a pageant coach, Tammy Caison, for the first time to assist me with the interview and proper pageant wardrobe.

When you have a great pageant coach who can dissect your bio with you—this is on the interview sheet given to judges—then you are prepared to answer any question that could be thrown at you. It's like walking into a test and already knowing every answer on the exam.

With a renewed sense of confidence, I felt great even though the stakes were high and the returning contestants had an edge with their experience.

Next, my coach showed me how to pick a wardrobe and color scheme that flattered me. You want to see the contestant shining in the clothes, not see the outfit itself. In my first pageant, I wore a gold dress on stage that washed me out with my blonde hair and fair skin. You couldn't really see me. But after working with my coach, I wore blue. When it came time for crowning, I won: Miss All American 2009.

It worked.

Three months later, I deployed to Iraq. While overseas, many of the other contestants with whom I had competed—even those I had beaten—sent me care packages. The pageant community is full of women who treat it all as more than just a crown on their heads.

Since 2009, I have been blessed to win: Ms. United America 2009, Ms. Texas United States 2012, Ms. United States 2012, Ms. Galaxy 2014, Ms. Earth 2018, and International Ms. 2020.

I earned these crowns while being stationed and deployed overseas as a naval officer. And serving with the title actually helped me to build my host nation relationships too while stationed in Japan and Italy. It was a terrific way to connect with the local communities.

Pageantry has brought me camaraderie, connection to traditions, and a wealth of knowledge about interpersonal relationships. Preparing for a pageant is tough. My days would start at 4:30 am with a solid workout at the gym (most people don't realize that we have to be in better shape for competitions than for military fitness tests). After the gym, it was a quick shower, and I was in uniform at work by 6:30 am. I would see patients all day with a break for lunch and occasional work meetings or trainings until 4 pm. After my workday ended, I often had one-on-one interview preparation with my coach.

Although it was tough, I realized that with anything in life, if something is important to you and you make it a priority, then you'll find a way to make it happen. Luckily, as long as I did my job well for the Navy and kept my pageant director in the loop, it all worked out nicely—albeit with an average of six hours of sleep per night.

Despite my successes, I have lost more pageants than I have won. Similarly, in life, you fail more times than you succeed.

But with each pageant, my courage grew. Courage to get in better shape. Courage to learn how to cook (so that I could eat healthy anywhere in the world). Courage to speak better. Courage to teach with empathy. Courage to navigate social media. Courage to shoot a video in a foreign country. And courage to juggle the demands of competing in a pageant while being true to my core mission as a naval officer and orthodontist.

In fact, competing in pageants did not detract from my mission in the military. Instead, it made me tougher, stronger, and a better communicator. It helped me build skills, relationships, and teams. It helped me grow.

To change and grow took courage. I knew I could either run from it or embrace it. Camaraderie, tradition, service, dedication, and discipline are traits of the military and pageantry.

(Queen photoshoot after winning Ms. United States 2012 — Photo by Ladd Photography)

Advice for All

"You get in life what you have the courage to ask for." —Oprah Winfrey

A stage is an outlet, a place where you can express your gifts and be challenged to stretch past your comfort zone. A stage can be a place to be your true self. If you let it, a stage can be where you push yourself beyond your comfort zone into something extraordinary.

As terrifying as it is to be on stage in front of others, how I got over the fear was that I knew I wasn't alone. Although many people were watching me, I knew that those same people were just like me: human, scared, nervous. I found safety in this. For me the stage felt like home because I was seen, I was safe, and I could project who I truly was through and through.

What's your stage? What's your passion? In pursuing it you have nothing to lose and everything to gain.

For me, my stage was competing and then winning a state, national, and international pageant while serving my country on active duty. It is important to find what stage works for you.

Perhaps your stage is a teacher in front of a classroom or being a parent at home with energetic kids or perhaps it is standing on top of a mountain after a long hike. Whatever it is, find that stage and own it.

We all have opportunities in our life when someone dares us to do something that we have never done. It can be scary. We may feel anxious, wondering if it's even possible. This is normal. Anything you do for the first time seems impossible like tying your own shoes, learning how to ride a bike, or making your bed with perfect square corners every single day in boot camp. But after you do it, again and again, you realize it isn't impossible; you were just discovering how to do it.

Think of one of the craziest things that you have always wanted to do but haven't tried yet. I dare you do it! I dare you to do it better.

You will either succeed or you won't. But you won't live your life with the regret of not going after what you want.

You have to make up your mind not to let people talk you out of it, not to let circumstances discourage you, and not to let naysayers drive you to give up.

Seek out coaches, mentors, and friends to help you achieve your goals. Realize too that you may outgrow some relationships as your mindset evolves. Be gracious and kind no matter what changes come.

You have to push harder than yesterday if you want a different tomorrow.

Don't rush the process; trust the process. Those who do things consistently and punctually surpass those who are naturally talented and gifted but don't follow through.

You have to believe in yourself and stay mentally tough. It's the only way through the b.s. in life.

Preparation is 90% of the work. Despite international time zone changes of 9-17 hours, I was always able to find a time to meet and connect with people who could help me achieve my goals. Like anything in life, if you are hungry and want it badly, you will find a way.

Advice for Pageants

"The extraordinary are fueled by why and the averages are always stuck with how." — Ed Mylett

If you can be one thing in life, be magnificent at getting better.

If you are competing in your first competition, do your homework. Research the pageant system and specific competition inside and out. This includes not only going to their website but also visiting all social media profiles and getting to know the current titleholders. Make sure it is a good fit.

Don't compete to get a crown on your head, compete only if you believe in the pageant's mission and you want to represent their values and purpose through your work as queen, should you win.

There's also a huge advantage to having a supportive director in large systems. She or he can be an advocate, ask the tough questions, and allow you to focus on the competition. The great ones I have had pushed me physically and mentally and ensured my hair and makeup were flawless on stage. It also allowed me to conserve my energy because sleep is your best friend during the weeklong competitions where you are in a constant state of adrenaline.

The week after a hefty competition, you will often experience a "pageant hangover." You will be able to eat your cheat meal, have a fun cocktail, and catch up on sleep. So focus on conserving your energy, eating clean, and prioritizing self-care throughout the competition so that the pageant hangover won't impact your day job.

Your drive to prove yourself and be the best will get you far. As soon as you win a crown or graduate from an academic program, you may tell yourself that you won't be happy until you achieve the next big thing. That's a dangerous cycle, so practice being in bliss. Be present and happy in each moment. And treat your crown win like a job that you embrace with humbleness and gratitude.

Surround yourself with people who cheer you on, not those who tell you your dreams are impossible or that you are wasting your time. When you doubt yourself, when you struggle, or when you need help you get back on your feet, those positive people will remind you that you've got this. Your mindset is the only thing to tweak, and others believe in you.

The biggest surprise I've discovered in pageantry is that it is leadership training, which helped me in the Navy. To be a good leader you have to be decisive, be confident, and know where you stand on current issues. You have to be ready at all times to handle tough questions and harsh critiques with dignity and grace. You will have to be resourceful, determined, and driven to succeed.

As Steve Jobs once said, "Management is about persuading people to do things they do not want to do, while leadership is about inspiring people to do things they never could."

Focus on what's good and what's on the horizon. Commit, care, and connect with your cause, organization, and the people within it. Be a reliable source of information and inspiration every day.

Be so good they can't ignore you.

To increase your influence as a leader, you must add value to others. Find what you do well. Look for what others do well. When you counsel people, you focus on their weaknesses; when you equip people, you focus on their strengths. Everyone has gifts and you must find them. Lean into your strengths and those of others. Support everyone and share your knowledge and network.

A sign of a good leader is that they make things happen; they are a catalyst. Adjust and be flexible. The playbook is being written in real-time, and you are an author.

Each one of us has faced obstacles in our lives but with the help of mentors, teachers, and coaches we can overcome them and turn these obstacles into gates of opportunity.

Everyone wants to win and to be a winner, but the difference between winners and spectators is that the winners have a belief that overrides the crowd's disbelief. Even though they have had failures and been knocked down, they find the intestinal fortitude to stand back up again to face the same challenge, learning from the previous mistakes and making it happen.

Winners fail a million times. What makes them winners is that nothing can stop them. There's no excuse for not being the hardest worker. Someone might be stronger, quicker, or younger, but you can still be the hardest worker.

Pageant queens are versatile, innovative, visionary trailblazers. If looks could kill, pageant women would be weapons of mass destruction. In pageantry, I'm thankful for my struggles because without them I wouldn't have stumbled across my strengths.

Be the woman you would look up to.

The best way to gain self-confidence is to do what you are afraid to do.

Someone's opinion of you does not have to become your reality. Your opinion of yourself is your reality.

To be glamorous in the pageant world, you have to put in the grind and sacrifices, endure the scrutiny, and cultivate your relentless drive for excellence.

You have an opportunity for rebirth. The dream is still alive in you. Take chances and don't be afraid to fail big and go outside the box.

The only person you need to be better than is the person you were yesterday.

Most of us had something in our childhoods that we were passionate about, that we loved, and that gave us something to look forward to. But as adults, our thought process changes. If the passion has no monetary value attached to it, we start thinking it doesn't matter anymore. Just because something doesn't make money doesn't mean it doesn't have value. Your passions, your dreams, and your goals have value because they matter to you.

What lights your heart on fire? You deserve to have a spark.

The biggest factors to your success are discipline, patience, and hard work.

As my father would always say, "Work smart, try hard, and never quit."

CHAPTER 5: JOINING THE NAVY

Timeline
Chapter 5

2005   In July, I attended Officer Development School (ODS) for five weeks.

2007   After graduating from dental school and taking my oath, I began work in the Navy in June.

2008

In November, I started my pre-deployment training with the Marines.

That Christmas would be the last my family shared all together for seven years.

2009   In February, I deployed to Iraq.

If you told my eight-year-old self that one day I would be in the Navy, as a dentist, deploying to the same part of the world as my dad, I would tell you that you were crazy. I never imagined that I would follow so closely in my father's footsteps. But I've learned in life to never say never because life is a roller coaster ride and it will surprise you.

After my first two years of dental school, I attended Officer Indoctrination School, now known as Officer Development School (ODS), in Newport, Rhode Island. For five weeks, I re-entered a world that was somewhat familiar from my childhood years walking around military bases. It was more intense now.

The chiefs would wake us up early with yelling and a lot of loud noise. I'd rush out of bed and feverishly throw on my physical training (PT) uniform of blue gym shorts and a white shirt with NAVY written on it. I stood at attention, burning a hole in the wall with my stare. Luckily, I didn't have a roommate in my room, so I slept on the bed not assigned to me—and would quickly stash the blanket and pillow I used underneath it—to ensure my bed was always perfectly made each morning.

The first week of ODS was a big adjustment, especially for my colleagues who were fighting caffeine withdrawal headaches since coffee was not served or allowed. We ate 10-minute meals three times a day and marched as a group to every class so no one was left behind.

I was part of the Papa Company and we did everything—and I mean everything—together. Our company was composed of dentists, nurses, lawyers, physicians, nuclear physicists (nicknamed "nukes"), and any other staff corps you can think of.

We had to jump in the water in our uniform to simulate life on a ship. Every week we would need to go to the uniform shop and spend our entire paychecks on repairing, tailoring, or replacing our uniforms to keep them up to standard. We practiced putting out fires, using gas masks, and running laps on the track all day long. Despite the ups and downs of ODS, we did everything as a team. We leaned on each other and we bonded through the challenges.

I was grateful my dad had told me to be prepared physically and mentally. I was already very active, but he reminded me that running, pushups, and sit-ups were focused on more in the Navy than in my workouts, so I focused there in advance. And I knew from growing up on military bases and having a father as a commander, when to speak and when to stand at attention. At the end of the day, I looked at it like a game, which was a helpful mentality. You had to practice, prepare, and be part of a team. It was tough so that we could learn and grow.

Six weeks later, we all graduated from ODS, and the majority of my classmates went into the fleet. I went back to dental school since this was the year 2005 and I had two years left.

After I graduated from dental school, I entered Naval Base San Diego, 32nd Street in June of 2007. This was the same place I had visited as a clerk and with my medical recruiter, but now I walked in as an officer and resident. I decided to do the Advanced Education in General Dentistry (AEGD) program that year. I knew that it was impossible to learn everything in dental school that I needed to know, and I was more confident in some areas than in others. I liked the idea of working with different specialists to build up my skills and my network. For one year in AEGD, I was able to focus on simply being a dentist.

My program director and first boss in the Navy was Commander Joe Molinaro. It was his first year as a program director too. He instantly made me feel comfortable and even called the other six residents and me "doc."

I was lucky that I knew one person in my class who came from UNLV dental school, Archie Gomez. We also completed ODS together in 2005. Although this place was already somewhat familiar, having another person there who knew me made it all the better.

In our resident room, there was a beat-up couch that was so comfortable you could instantly fall asleep on it the moment you sat down, a large table, and a computer screen. This room became the place where lectures were given by attendees and Navy leadership—from the commanding officer to the detailer, all people who would have a significant impact on our career. When we weren't in lectures the resident room was a place where we could hang out, let our hair down, and just be.

Every day we would arrive at the base at 06:45 in our uniforms where we would change into scrubs and see patients. Sometimes I felt like I changed five times a day since the Navy has so many uniforms—different ones for work, service, service dress, ceremonial, dinner dress, and training. These uniforms also differ for officers, Chief Petty Officers, and enlisted members who are E6 and below. So, we would change from our khaki uniform to our scrubs then back to khakis then to dress blues then to scrubs then to gym clothes. If we drove to another place, we would need to change and the necessary uniform would be dictated by where we were going and with whom we were speaking.

About halfway through the year, Commander Molinaro allowed us to arrive in gym clothes and change once there. His decision may have been in part to having coffee spilled on him in the car once a week on his commute, or that my classmates always walked in with coffee stains on their pants. As the only female in my class, I also faced some wardrobe issues like when my belt was backward or the bottom of my shoes crumbled as I walked. One of our classmates always seemed to put his devices in the wrong place too. We were always there to help him though—we grew together as residents and also bonded with our boss. I was especially honored when Commander Molinaro welcomed us into his home; I loved meeting his family. This was the Navy I wanted to be a part of, where people come first.

In my class of residents, some were single, others were married, and a few already had kids. Despite being at different stages of life, we all understood, respected, and bonded with each other. During our year we rotated to the other bases to work with different mentors. One of my favorites was going to the base Marine Corps Recruit Depot (MCRD) where I extracted wisdom teeth.

Our patients at MCRD were recruits in the middle of boot camp to become Marines. One of their requirements was to have any wisdom teeth extracted that had the potential to flare up. In a systematic fashion, we would blindfold them (to protect their eyes and help them to relax) and numb the area with local anesthesia. We played music in the background and I found new ways to help them understand the difference between pressure and pain.

I didn't get to extract a lot of teeth in dental school, so it was wonderful to get hands-on practice in a quick and efficient way. Working with our mentors, they would do one side of the jaw and I would do the other. As my confidence grew, I would handle entire cases by myself and then have my mentor review at the end to ensure I was carrying out the procedure the best I could. To make my patients feel more involved, I had them help me by pushing into me to bite down. At the end of the procedure, I had them sit up, gave them pain medicine (and antibiotics, if needed), and told their instructor to let them rest. Sometimes these drill sergeants would listen and sometimes they wouldn't, which was evident during a recruit's post-op appointment.

The recruits we worked on were mostly teenage kids—some were forced to join the military by their parents, others just wanted to get out of where they were from, and some never had three square meals a day growing up, let alone a visit to the dentist, because their parents couldn't afford it. Many of my patients confided in me that they joined the military to get access to healthcare, be able to see a dentist, eat better, and be a part of something bigger than themselves.

I remember the MCRD feeling like the movie Platoon where the drill sergeants saluted and barked orders indoors. One time a drill sergeant came back to check on his recruit in my dental chair. He pushed the blindfolded recruit and boomed loudly, "Get ready! Doc is going to rip out all your teeth!"

I was nervous and unsure what to do or say since I had only been in the Navy for four weeks and had never had someone outside our crew come into our space to poke around.

Luckily, my corpsman (my dental assistant) stepped in and said, "You get out of here. Now is no time to tease this young man."

The drill sergeant looked surprised. My corpsman was one-half his size, but her spirit and conviction more than made up for the difference in physical stature. This was the first time I saw what military bearing looked like: standing your ground with 100% confidence and unwavering certainty.

He didn't move, so she continued, "If you don't leave right away, I will strap you down and start taking out your teeth—starting with the ones in the front."

To my relief, he shrugged and left.

Later, she told me that some drill sergeants liked to come in unannounced like they owned the place to "check on their recruits," when actually they were just trying to take advantage of their vulnerable state and intimidate them. It was then I knew what it meant to stand up for your patients.

After two weeks of hands-on practice with my mentors who were both exodontists (experienced dentists who specialize in teeth extraction), my confidence and speed soared. They taught me how to work safely, efficiently, and methodically for patients.

Yet reality hit me when I realized that the patients I got to practice with were young, healthy 18-year-olds with soft bones. So I couldn't get too overconfident because cases in other populations would not always be so easy—bone becomes significantly harder after age 25.

Two months later I faced a big challenge when I was back at my home base at 32nd Street taking out a wisdom tooth of a 38-year-old African American Chief whose bone was as tough as a brick wall. In the middle of the procedure, the power went out. No lights, no suction, and not much time before the anesthesia would wear off. I had a battery-powered headlamp, so I tried to work fast. Luckily, Captain Smith, a Navy oral surgeon and my mentor, was next to me and was able to assist so I could finish the procedure despite the curveballs. It was the hardest extraction I've had, even to this day.

These experiences shaped me as a dentist and as a Naval officer. I was starting to learn my strengths and limitations. Learning how to be a good dentist and Naval officer was a juggle for me all the time, but I was always committed to improving.

CDR Molinaro told me he was grateful to be my first leader and that he would push me hard because he believed in me. He expected more of me every day and wouldn't ask me to do something he wouldn't do himself. He encouraged camaraderie among my peers and me and encouraged us to look out for each other.

During that first year in the Navy, I also volunteered to be the Chairperson for Children's Dental Health Month. My classmates and I collected supplies and were able to reach 5,000 children, teaching them the importance of oral healthcare. It felt good to be back in my element with kids, although I have to admit that many of my adult patients were adult kids at heart.

I also did a rotation with the orthodontist Commander Scott Curtice who I had met during my clerkship the previous year. Ironically, our fathers were both in the Navy Dental Corps at the same time when their service years overlapped too. Dr. Curtice's kindness, generosity, and mentorship helped me believe that I could be an orthodontist in the military—despite the obstacles.

Very often, I was seen as just a pretty girl and nothing more. Many doctors blew me off or wouldn't acknowledge that I was even in the room. Dr. Curtice never made me feel this way and even stood up for me when the other orthodontist stationed at the 32nd Street base said they didn't like me. Later when I got into residency, he bragged about it to everyone, even to the officers who had scoffed at the idea.

I learned so much working with Dr. Curtice, including the importance of building relationships with not only my patients but also with their chain of command and other dental providers. I saw too that I didn't have to give up who I was with a cheerful, energetic, and outgoing persona to do this job in the Navy.

"You have the personality of an orthodontist," Dr. Curtice said to me once. This was the same thing another mentor had told me in dental school.

"What is the personality of an orthodontist?"

"An orthodontist is high-energy, extroverted, and playful, yet also pristine and polished in their appearance and demeanor. They are able to juggle many things at once and make people feel important, appreciated, and valued in the chair. Orthodontists are all about relationships since we have our patients for two years or longer."

"So true!"

"These are all things that come naturally to you," he said kindly.

Maybe the Universe was trying to tell me something.

The following month I worked with Captain Smith, an oral maxillofacial surgeon at my home base. He was a jokester but loved to teach. We always joked that he would push me hard in the clinic—by asking me tough questions and having me figure out cases on my own with him waiting until I'm ready to give up before he would come in to help—and then I would do the same at the gym for him or anyone who came to work out during lunch. I would push and encourage people to get better and grill them on ab exercises, circuit training, or any area I wanted to focus on.

One day, a patient walked in with a unique bite we described as Skeletal and Dental Class III. In other words, her skeletal and dental jaws didn't fit and gave the appearance of a protruding chin and an underbite. She had been seeing an orthodontist for five years, but this was the first time Dr. Smith had seen her. I was intrigued because I never knew patients could have braces for that long or that surgery was an option for this type of issue.

Dr. Smith helped me fill out a referral for her to an orthognathic board (a place where oral surgeons, orthodontists, and general dentists met to discuss corrective jaw surgery cases). I asked if I could go to the orthognathic board where her case would be presented to the team of dentists. I wanted to learn more. This was the dark side of orthodontics: surgery, an operating room, going under the knife. And I fell in love with it.

Orthognathic surgery, as it is called, can be a game-changer for so many of my patients because the cost is covered by the military and it is conducted by a talented team of surgeons who do numerous cases. Because of the high cost, these surgeries are not often seen outside the military or academic setting.

Once my rotations were complete for my AEGD residency, I asked for extra time in both orthodontics and oral surgery because I wanted to explore these areas more. I had never had braces myself and didn't know orthodontics was capable of working with a team to achieve extraordinary things.

I quickly learned that getting into residency in orthodontics is incredibly challenging in the Navy, so I knew I had to find a way to stand out.

Upon graduation from my AEGD residency, I transferred to Marine Corps Air Station Miramar and informed my leadership I wanted to deploy. I knew an operational tour would not only make me a better clinician but also a better leader and officer. So I raised my hand to go to the Middle East.

In November 2008, I started my pre-deployment training with the Marines. It was grueling. I had to up my game significantly both physically and mentally. Everything considered to be a size "small" in the Marines—like gear and clothing—was huge on me.

On one obstacle course, the Marine Sergeant just glided from one bar to the next and hopped over the walls like they were small puddles in the ground. At 5'3" I couldn't reach the first bar on the course and had to take a leap of faith that I wouldn't fall or injure myself.

I hadn't told my parents about deployment because I knew I would break down and cry. I knowingly volunteered to put myself in danger and was terrified of the unknown. I would be leaving beautiful Southern California to go to a country that treated women as second-class citizens and was known for uncharted and deadly minefields.

When you combine anxiety and uncertainty you get fear. But I knew I needed to walk with my fear because it was the right thing to do. As I worked through the hump (a several-mile hike), gas mask training, field training, and numerous immunizations, I had to wrestle with the emotions that threatened to engulf me: excitement, fear, anxiousness, uncertainty, pride, nervousness, anticipation. I had no idea what I signed up to do but knew I wanted to be part of something bigger than myself.

During Field Marine Officer School (FMOS), a part of pre-deployment, we had to go through an obstacle course full of smoke, barbed wire, and walls that looked impossible to climb. Our corpsmen went through the same course simultaneously. I can remember them finishing the obstacle courses before us and then cheering us officers on. We were building our camaraderie with and trust for each other before we left on deployment. I can still remember taking the elbow guards and using them on my knees since the knee guards were too big for my small stature. As I crawled under the barbed wire and then into swampy water, I felt the mud go through my uniform all the way into my pants, leaving no surface untouched.

A few concussions and twisted ankles later, I was able to make it over the walls in each part of the obstacle course and kept smiling. My Marine instructors took note of that. They knew we would be their doctors and felt that if we put 110% effort into everything, they would do the same for us, including catching our bullets if we were ever in harm's way during deployment.

That same December, my cousin Carl (who was in the Army Reserve) and my brother (petty officer 2nd class in the Navy submarine community) also told my family they were deploying in 2009. It would be our last Christmas together for seven years.

I was grateful I had some family nearby who could help me pack my things, mail a small box of stuff (like photos, holiday decor, favorite snacks, magazines, and anything to cheer up my crew once on location), and take me to the airport. Since my parents were in Nevada and owned their own business, it was hard for them to come to see me off. Plus, we never knew when I was actually leaving. Thankfully, my Aunt Barbara and Uncle RE were still in the area and drove me to the air terminal at U.S. Air Force Base Riverside, California when the time finally came in February 2009. Both nervous and excited for me, my Uncle told me to get ready for the biggest adventure in my life. Then he and my aunt waved goodbye. I didn't know it yet, but he was right.

My team had another female officer, Commander Brooks, this was the one thing I asked my executive officer to have on my deployment in addition to the four corpsmen. As we sat on the cold floor and waited 12 hours for our flight, we watched military war movies like Saving Private Ryan, Band of Brothers, Flag of Our Fathers, and Braveheart to get us pumped for what could happen next.

When our plane arrived, I realized we were the only passengers. This was a first for me. I had never been on a flight with solely military members, especially with just Navy and Marines only. It was my Combat Logistics Battalion and that was it—no civilians. This just added to the gravity of the situation and the reality that deployment was happening. To be honest, I was feeling pretty nervous, but also incredibly excited.

Ammunition from our guns was emptied and stored below the plane with the cargo. Our flight attendants were incredibly kind; we never went hungry. Each time we stopped, the flight team would rotate out. We didn't have enough time to leave the airport, so there was a lot of sitting and waiting, but the unknown of where we were going next kept us excited.

Our plane flew from Riverside, California to Rockwall, Illinois to Bangor, Maine to Iceland to Frankfurt, Germany, and then to Kuwait. We flew for over 22 hours. Upon landing, we were rushed off the plane and into a bus with all windows blocked off. It was the middle of the night and we couldn't see anything. Quickly but quietly, we arrived at our base and I hit the cot hard.

Upon waking the next morning, the blinding sun made the sand all around glimmer. We were in the middle of nowhere. The sand slipped right through our fingers, it was so fine. It felt different than anything I felt before; it was not like the sand on the beaches in

California and Hawaii. It was like we were on the moon but with normal gravity. I didn't know what to think.

That day we were told that we would be there for the next week or so until we could get on another flight to Iraq. Three days later, we left in the middle of a sandstorm. Heading out, I couldn't see my hand in front of me. How can the pilots see where we are going?

As we loaded into the cargo plane, we sat facing each other, knees touching. It was the first time since starting deployment training that I felt grateful to be small. This was the epitome of an adventure. I closed my eyes and prayed. You could cut the tension and anticipation in the air with a knife. Was this what I signed up for when I swore that I would serve my country?

Yes.

(Left: Pre-deployment training at Field Medical Officer School, Camp Pendleton, California. Right: As a newly promoted Commander in the United States Navy at USS Midway in San Diego, California in 2019 — Photo by Arielle Levy Photography)

Advice

Listen to your heart. I know it's risky, but take that leap of faith.

You must train your mindset. The optimal performers in the military have mastered this concept in every community. You must have the mindset of a lion—they are not the fastest, but their mentality and strength make them King. Your 'can' must be larger than your 'cannot.'

Resiliency is incredibly important. You have to bounce back no matter what challenges you face.

You can feel scared but act bravely anyway. Acknowledge your fragility but come back stronger. Introspection, reflection, and self-evaluation are tools to help you stretch outside your comfort zone and grow.

Camaraderie is a universal theme in the military no matter your rank, the service you belong to, the community you claim, or the profession you hold. If you are active, a reserve, or a veteran, camaraderie is vital. We can't grow as a person or as a team until we shed trauma and heal. Often this work includes others. Vulnerability and open, honest communication are the keys to maintaining the foundation of the company you are part of. The ego fades away.

Relationships with others, and with ourselves, play a huge role in our happiness. As psychotherapist and *New York Times* bestselling author Esther Perel says, "The quality of our life is determined by the quality of our relationships." Friendships give you the energy to break through obstacles, the courage to push past your comfort zone, and the wisdom to expand to new levels of growth. We all need people in our life who have our backs and who remind us that we are better, we deserve more, and we can do more than what we think is possible.

Give yourself time and space to process and heal. In the military, we are given pre-deployment, deployment, and post-deployment time and training. We are given time to prepare and time to recover from a life-changing experience. Know what your mission is, know what your intent is as the commander in your life, and then fight with everything you've got to win.

Leadership is a skill that has to be learned and fostered. It must come from a place of wanting to serve. This is seen at every level in the military. Move people with your gratitude, appreciation, and dedication to helping others win. Don't try to push through your agenda with the rank on your shoulder. A leader's job is not to do the work of others; it is to help others learn how to do it themselves and to succeed beyond what they thought possible. At the same time, a leader is never seen waiting to be told what to do next. Take initiative. The ability to learn is the most important quality a leader can possess. Yet, a leadership role is not the only way to have a profound impact, so see the value in what each person brings to the table, no matter their position.

Monitor your energy. Think about the energy you give to people, the energy you give to social media, and the energy you give to yourself. Are you sharpening your blade or are you sitting back and letting it go dull?

Hard times reveal true character. Are you going to sink or are you going to swim? Obstacles in life are there to help teach you how to swim.

As Muhammad Ali said, "I hated every minute of training, but I said, 'Don't quit. Suffer now and live the rest of your life as a champion.'"

CHAPTER 6:
DEPLOYED IN IRAQ

Timeline
Chapter 6

2009

In February, I deployed to Iraq.

In early summer, I learned I was selected to go into orthodontics by the Navy. My Tri-Service Orthodontic Residency Program (TORP) would begin in June 2010.

In September, our replacements arrived, and I headed home.

A week later, I started post-deployment training in San Diego and began to go through reverse culture shock.

2010

In June, I began TORP in San Antonio, Texas.

I opened my eyes, and we landed roughly. The Executive Officer (XO) of the combat logistics battalion unit CLB-7 at Al Asad greeted us. Located in the Al Anbar province—at the time, the deadliest zone in Iraq—Al Asad was our new home base. This was our unit.

It was now the middle of the night, and our XO was happy we arrived safely in spite of the insane weather storm. Apparently, when we left Kuwait the pilots flew above the storm, but it got far worse upon entering Iraq air space with very little visibility. After the quick greeting, we made our way to our berthing, the place where we would stay, and met the group we were replacing. To say they were glad to see us was an understatement. They were relieved we were safe but also happy to be able to go home.

None of us had taken a real shower in about a week and we were anxious to do so. As we walked into our spaces, my corpsmen jumped up and down with glee. As seasoned dental assistants, they had more operational experience under their belts and didn't see a beaten-down building but a hardened structure where each of us could have our own rooms instead—a true luxury on deployment. They were happy to get an upgrade from previous deployments.

I took over the lieutenant's room after he left and found all sorts of hidden treasures like Herbal Essences shampoo, magazines, and board games. I surmised from these items that a female officer must have been here before Lieutenant Paul Kocian relieved her. He just pushed everything to the back of the closets and drawers, which I later discovered. I knew I could decorate and make this room my sanctuary, so I began a scavenger hunt through my room, the rest of our building, and abandoned buildings on base. I went to find things like mattress pads, American flags, extension cords, and anything else I could repurpose to make my place feel like home.

I had lots of support from my family, friends, and pageant girlfriends who sent me care packages often. In one care package, my mom sent me my brother's old sheets that were perfect to sleep on. Enclosed in another package were photos from my phone that I used to make a collage on my wall. It cheered me up whenever I looked at it. I found an American flag that was perfect to cover the large hole on my wall next to the door—we were stationed in a former Iraqi base that had been bombed many times.

One weekend, my boss, our psychologist, and I decided to go on a scavenger hunt within our base. As one of the top nine countries with the most uncharted minefields in the world, Iraq had numerous hidden dangers, so mapping our course ahead of time was crucial to our survival. We found abandoned buildings with mattress pads, desks, and other useful items that we brought back safely, but I learned quickly to stay on marked paths. However, the path markers could move easily during sandstorms. When you're in a war zone you have to put one foot in front of the other, never knowing if it could be your last step.

Our dental clinic was austere, and I did not always have all the instruments or supplies that I needed to get the job done, so I learned to be creative in doing my best with what I had. Plus, when you are on a base of 25,000 soldiers in the middle of a dangerous sandbox, something is bound to happen. From wiring a guy's broken jaw shut in the middle of the night with my oral surgeon to doing a root canal with a paperclip to using fishing string to save a Marine's front teeth—improvising was just part of my job.

In the States, supplies were plentiful and you always had electricity and running water, but we were deep in Iraq, a war-torn and impoverished country. Many people literally had nothing. The only gear or supplies we had were what others left behind or what we brought over.

I was incredibly lucky to be at a larger base though because many of the patients I saw came from forward operating bases (FOBs). These areas were so small and remote that they showered from a bag of water and ate only MREs (meals ready to eat). When I learned this, I would purposely stretch my procedures so they could have a decent night of sleep, a shower, and food from our facilities.

During my time in Iraq, I had the pleasure of working with Army dentists as well who shared with me how they would figure things out and just make it work. Many of my colleagues had similar experiences and we built a network that enabled us to share our bag of tricks with each other.

Constant cleaning was also necessary because of the amount of sand that leaked in everywhere. We put tape around windows and towels next to the doors in the clinic to seal it at night, but the sand was persistent. I remember unpacking my seabag (a duffel bag carried by sailors and marines) and was shocked that the sand got into my clothes despite being packed inside a Ziploc bag inside a garbage bag inside my seabag.

Even though it got as hot as 130 degrees Fahrenheit outside, we were required to be in our uniform no matter where we went. So, I was grateful for the gym where I could wear shorts and for my shower where I could cool off. The water was not potable, so it was unsafe to drink but okay to shower in. Although I questioned even that since it looked yellow going down the drain. Bottled water was everywhere, and we used it for brushing our teeth and I used it to wash my face too. Laundry was taken and done for us once a week. Finding a routine gave me a sense of normalcy.

Being on deployment you become grateful for things that you never thought you would be grateful for. Hearing music on a radio, holding real silverware in your hand, using a toilet that flushes, or being able to drive a car and just go wherever you want—these were all luxuries that I no longer had.

On my first day in the clinic, I met Lieutenant Payton Fennel, the medical doctor of the Command Battalion who ran the base medical clinic. He was charming and kind. I instantly felt a connection with him, and he quickly became my battle buddy. A battle buddy is like your best friend—someone who looks out for you, checks in on you, and makes sure you are doing okay. They are invested in you as much as you are in them. During times of conflict, coupled with no family support system and only ourselves, it was crucial for us both to have each other. In Fennel's office was a picture of his wife Chris and their daughter Ryann. Stunning.

I learned he had two more young sons too, one of whom was born in 2008 right before he left. I could see the toll it took on him to be so far away from his family. He shared with me that they had to let go of the nanny because he couldn't earn as much while deployed as when stateside, and his kids were often cooped up inside. So, we put together care packages to send to them. I knew all too well what it was like to have my father away on deployment and receive things that showed he loved and thought of me.

Work in our clinic felt like feast or famine; some days we were slammed with a ton of patients and other days it was empty. Either way, we were always on call and had to be ready to take care of any sailor, marine, or soldier who walked into our dental clinic in pain. My first patient was a Colonel in the Iraqi Security Force (ISF). He was accompanied by a translator who looked me up and down, shook his head, and asked for the dentist.

"I am the dentist."

"We want a male dentist," the translator said.

"There aren't any male dentists here. My boss is a female too if you'd like to speak with her."

After an exchange of words in Farsi, the ISF Colonel sat down in my chair. He opened his mouth, and I was dumbfounded. It looked like a pinball arcade machine where the metal ball had run amok in his mouth. His chipped teeth were covered in black and brown stains, his gums were recessed, and the stench that the decay made reminded me of a dirty diaper. I had no idea which tooth was causing him pain since there were so many suspects. When he pointed to the tooth that was most painful, it was actually one that looked the least damaged.

After my clinical exam, I discovered he had localized aggressive periodontal disease, which is a rare form of inflammatory periodontal disease that spreads fast and causes severe bone loss. It was one of my easiest extractions. Because the tooth was so mobile due to the periodontal disease, it practically fell out on its own.

When the extraction was complete, I stood up and sand slid off my camouflage pants. I prescribed him antibiotics to prevent infection, which was the best I could do for him with our limited resources.

He nodded but said nothing. The translator thanked me, and they left. I never saw him again.

At the clinic, just like in our home, we had to clean a lot. My boss, Commander Brooks, and I liked organization and couldn't stand all the sand that leaked into the clinic. We also gathered up unneeded supplies to trade with other groups on other bases or doctors on deployment in other areas in the Middle East. We kept only what we needed and gave away or swapped what we didn't need.

WiFi was slow, computers were scarce, and electrical power outages were common. One day when I turned the power strip off, the cord caught on fire. I was able to stop it rather quickly but getting the support team to come out to fix it seemed impossible. That was of course until I told them I had the automatic external defibrillator (AED) plugged into it and it was no longer charging. They came to my clinic within minutes after that, knowing this life-saving tool was essential.

Many of the materials and products we used in dental clinics could ruin my uniform if they came into contact, so I had my mom send me scrub tops. They had flowers, cartoon characters like Garfield, teddy bears, and every bright color you could imagine. It drove the Marines crazy, but it wasn't like I could go buy new uniforms, and they knew it. Because my uniforms were a prize possession, I wanted to ensure they stayed in the best shape possible. So, cheerful and silly scrubs it was.

One day, I had a patient come in who didn't have a weapon. This was not the norm. On deployment, each of us was issued a 9mm Beretta to carry at all times. When I came into the clinic, I had taken mine off to see patients. My assistant Hospital Corpsman 3rd Class (HM3) Pagart got really quiet.

He motioned for me to meet him in my office and said, "Doc, this guy must have done something really bad. They just don't take away someone's weapon."

I nodded and said, "Do not leave the room while the sailor is in there, okay?"

He agreed, and we went back into the room. As I evaluated the patient, he began to do something that I had never experienced. He wrapped his mouth around my two fingers that were holding a mirror to see inside his mouth. Taken aback, I quickly told him to knock it off. I was grateful that my corpsman was there too. He said a few words to the patient that I would rather not repeat, but I was thankful I was not alone. That was the first time I had ever felt violated by a patient. After we finished his treatment, we learned he was facing several military charges under the Uniformed Code of Military Justice.

From that day on, I made sure I was never in the room treating my patients alone.

One of the best parts of deployment was the fact we were able to work with other branches of service. The Army had a hospital set up next door to us and they loved having themed barbecue events like a Hawaiian luau and an 80's party. They had a different culture from what I grew up with and became accustomed to in the Navy, but I really enjoyed it. They even connected me with the chefs in the chow hall who were happy to make cakes for my corpsmen who celebrated their birthdays on deployment.

There were also two dentists in the Army crew—a general dentist and an oral surgeon. The oral surgeon, Major Mark Ranschart, taught me a lot. He was the only oral surgeon for the Al Anbar region. One day, his tech woke me up to come to assist with wiring a Marine's jaw shut. We needed to stabilize his broken jaw so that it would heal properly and prevent severe complications in the future. Another time, I placed a splint to save a Marine's front tooth. Who would have guessed that a bullet to the face could be stopped by a tooth?

Major Ranschart showed me how to be compassionate and caring with my patients in an especially stressful environment. I was still very green in the dentistry field and helping with cases far more complicated than anything I'd been exposed to in school. Plus, these Marines were trained not to express emotion or complain, so sometimes diagnosis was not as easy as back home. The Major demonstrated how to masterfully treat others no matter the limitations we faced. He and I are still friends today.

Happiness and success depended on us. We were a team that worked together towards a common vision to help those we served. That was the fuel that drove us to think outside the box, be resourceful, and never give up to achieve outstanding results. We made the most of deployment. The truth is our mistakes don't limit us, only our fears do.

Deployment days were long, but the weeks went by fast. On Memorial Day weekend, our chow hall was decorated with everything American imaginable. I was excited that a care package from my family came in too. I got sunglasses, headbands, and décor that I could put up in the clinic to help my corpsmen get their minds off what they were missing back home. This year we didn't want to see fireworks (also used as a sign for incoming bombs) or fires (never a good idea in a sweltering desert with limited water)— we just wanted to be. We played golf and basketball. We ate a ton of good food. It was a great day.

A few weeks later, the temperatures reached a record high of 135 Fahrenheit and several sandstorms hit. They arrived like waves pummeling the shore but with many colors, from orange to pitch black. After each one, I felt like I had gotten an intense exfoliation. I guess I'm good on microdermabrasion for the next few years.

I never knew sandstorms like that existed. They were intense, and we felt like we were in a movie, not real life. I was grateful for my place but thought of colleagues, sailors, and other Marines on forward operating bases. When they came to see me, I stretched their treatment so they could get a hot meal and a shower, something they didn't always get depending on where they were located.

I also found my dental chair becoming a therapy chair, where my patients could vent and I would just listen. It wasn't what I expected from my deployment, but I was happy to know I could be there for them. Sometimes what I heard or saw took a toll on me. I didn't know who I could go to, so I was grateful to have my battle buddy; Lieutenant Fennell and I checked in on each other daily.

His deployment extended from six months to a year when his replacement became pregnant and there was no one to relieve him. I remember the day he got the news; he was frustrated because he missed his family and hadn't expected to be gone that long. I comforted him, listened, and told him we needed to do what would cheer him up. The gym was one of the things that did that.

Lieutenant Fennell loved staying healthy and was planning on completing a Sports Medicine fellowship upon returning to the states. He taught me how to use the gym equipment, a concept foreign to me since previously I had just done cardio exercises to stay in shape. I started working out twice a day and learned from Fennell how to lift properly and how to get the most out of my workouts. Learning good technique helped me not feel intimidated around all guys, which was huge for my self-esteem. I felt stronger both internally and externally. I became even more confident in who I was and felt even more part of my team.

Another of our friends, Army Captain Nathan Carlson, was an incredible runner. When running a speedy 12mph on the treadmill, he looked like he was just casually jogging. At a United States Marine Corps (USMC) marathon, Nathan ran it in record time, averaging a 4.30-mile. This was in dry 100-degree heat.

I was grateful for these two officers, and we shared many nights telling stories, watching movies, or reading the bible together. I was actually raised Catholic and pressured by my father to go to church, but never felt fully connected, especially when I saw so many people preaching one thing and behaving poorly. As I became an adult I gravitated to non-denominational churches. In reading the bible with my friends, having long talks, and hearing the story of Esther (a beauty queen who saved her people), I felt a renewed pull toward Christianity. They showed me new ways to think about religion and how to make it applicable to life. I learned that God is the CEO in my life.

A week into summer, I received the best news: I was selected to go into orthodontics by the Navy. I quickly readied my applications, thinking through how the required interviews would go. Because I was on deployment on the other side of the world, my interview happened at 2 am. I sat in the hallway of my berthing where I had complete silence. Everyone else was asleep, and only adrenaline was keeping me awake. I answered all the questions about who I was, what I wanted to bring to the program, and what I hoped my legacy in the Navy orthodontic community would be. It went fast and 15 minutes later I was done and off to bed. However, I couldn't sleep because of the anticipation and nerves.

A week later, I was offered a spot at Tri-service Orthodontic Residency Program (TORP) at Lackland Air Force Base in San Antonio, Texas. Thousands of people from the Army, Air Force, and Navy apply for only two to five spots per year, so I couldn't believe I got in but enthusiastically accepted. My battles working through test anxiety in dental school, asking for extra rotations in orthodontics, and volunteering for deployment all paid off.

The program would not begin for me until the following year in June 2010, but I started messaging the Navy residents there immediately. I wanted to learn, read, study, and connect as much as I could before I arrived. One person I connected with early was Rasha who was a first-year resident. I was thrilled that she acted as my sponsor and shared what she was learning in Texas with me in Iraq via email so I'd have a bit of an idea of what to expect when I arrived the following summer.

Speaking of summer, in Iraq, summertime was brutal. One day I was outside the wire visiting a local Iraqi camp, and it was 130 degrees Fahrenheit. The Marine unit I was with had recovered weapons from insurgents before escorting several other doctors and me through. The Staff Sargent in charge asked if we wanted to shoot the weapons since the ammunition in them had to be fully discharged before we returned back to base.

Of course, we said yes but had no clue how to use them. So, the Marine security unit set up a range and secured the area to ensure we were the only ones there. As we lined up in front of the range, they handed us AK-47 semi-automatic rifles. The range master instructed us to push the side lever down one click. This meant when we pulled the trigger, only one shot should fire.

However, when we shot, lots of bullets came blasting out. These AK-47s were not high-quality, US-standard weapons and were calibrated differently since they didn't go through the regulations and safety checks that our weapons went through. Despite our surprise, the range master told us to keep shooting.

It was challenging since the guns were heavy, difficult to control, and like nothing we are accustomed to (our daily carry was a much smaller 9mm pistol). As we shot, the back of the weapon hit hard into my shoulder, again and again. The flak jacket (bulletproof vest) that I wore was too big, and the weapon holster had been removed. Cheered on by my fellow sailors and Marines to finish the magazine of bullets, I muscled through the shoulder pain.

After we finished firing all the ammunition, we high-fived and headed back to the main base. Back in my room when I removed my gear, I found that I had a large bruise on my right shoulder where the skin was pulled and stretched by the gun's kickback. It was swollen and had already turned various colors of purple, black, and yellow.

Another doctor deployed with us was a dermatologist, so I asked if he could sew my shoulder up. I knew that if the scar did not heal properly, I would be self-conscious about it. That scar would become a proud reminder of my time on deployment for the rest of my life.

When the weather cooled down and fall arrived in September, so did my unit's replacement. The demographics of the base were changing from Marine to Army and the shift of the wartime efforts was moving from Iraq to Afghanistan for Operation Enduring Freedom. I couldn't believe my time there was coming to an end.

I spent the last night with my battle buddy, watching The Notebook and journaling. A true friend can remind you of the songs in your heart when you have forgotten the words. I didn't want to say goodbye. It was bittersweet. On one hand, I was excited to go home, see old friends and family, and enjoy the small luxuries I missed. On the other hand, I had become accustomed to the less complicated, mission-driven world we were in and had found safety in it.

But life goes on, and we have to keep moving forward too.

Our journey home was far less eventful than the plane ride there. We stopped in Ireland, Maine, and then California. When my Aunt Barbara greeted me at Camp Pendleton, I wasn't sure if she would recognize me. For seven months, I had worn the same clothes day in and out, hadn't seen a hairdresser, and knew my body was different after the twice-a-day workouts in the gym. But my aunt did recognize me, and I couldn't help getting teary-eyed when she reached out her arms to give me a hug. We were also greeted by many members of the dental battalion.

My parents flew in later that day from Reno, and Mexican food was what I craved the most for my first meal back. However, after seven months of eating that bland and spice-less military chow, my stomach wasn't too happy about it.

The following week, I started post-deployment training and experienced much of what my father used to go through upon his returns: culture shock, adapting, and adjusting to 'normal' life. I no longer had someone who did my laundry, cooked all my meals, or cleaned my bathroom. I had to re-learn these habits. Even driving on the freeway was a shock to my system. I hadn't driven or listened to the radio in seven months and with the fast pace of civilian life, it seemed like I was on a hamster wheel playing catchup at warp speed.

During our post-deployment training at Camp Pendleton in San Diego, I looked at the dental team who had come with me on deployment and I was filled with gratitude. They say deployment changes you and the people you meet become lifelong friends. They were right. I learned how to make do with limited resources during my time in the Middle East. And my teammates helped me grow.

Because some friends and family members were still deployed and waiting to go home, I reached out. For example, I wrote to my battle buddy and sent him care packages since he was there till Christmas. He was at his breaking point, and I hoped some surprises in the mail would help.

After deployment, Fennel left the Navy to fulfill his dreams as a Sports Medicine physician with his own practice and is now a team doctor for a hockey team in North Carolina. My friend Nathan left the Army and remained a physical therapist for the military, working as a civilian. My colleague Mark left the Army and opened up private practice in Prosper, Texas. As for me, I was off to orthodontics residency and left for San Antonio, Texas in May of 2010.

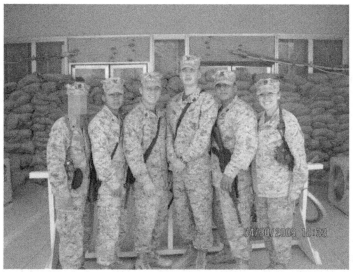

(April 2009: Camp Al Asaad, Iraq, Navy Dental Team. Left to right: CAPT Brooks (blurred), HM3 Servando Quinones, HM3 Joseph Pagart, HM3 Joel Tatum, HM2 Fernando Abundis, and me LT)

Advice

Don't live with regret — go after your dreams. Any problems or failures you encounter become gifts once you learn from them.

Accept what is. In order to love who you are, you cannot hate the experiences that shaped you.

Reframe things to your advantage. You have the power to choose the meaning you attach to an event. What are you focusing on? Figure out a solution. Don't complain or focus on things that are disempowering. Our brains are question answering machines, so ask good questions. Focus on what you can control. How can I grow from this? What are the opportunities in this situation?

Change is the only constant. We are in a constant state of evolution and flux. Changes come with every command you lead and every new boss you have. Technology is growing exponentially. The world changes each day. Welcome change and adapt to it. Stay open-minded to the possibilities that change can bring.

Honor, courage, and commitment. These are the Navy Core Values. Be proud of who you are and what you stand for. Having courage doesn't mean you don't get afraid, it means you don't let fear stop you. You walk with fear and are committed to yourself, your team, and your unit to complete your mission. Finish what you started and do it well.

Things happen *for* you, not *to* you. Everything can be scary but look at fear, embrace it, and empower yourself to take control so that it does not control you.

Believe in yourself. You are in control of what you accept. You have a choice. Success is nothing more than a few simple disciplines practiced every day.

Struggle is necessary. Everyone who is struggling right now needs to understand this: what you are going through is necessary. It's necessary because you are forging the skills, the determination, the grit, the drive, and the passion that no one standing still can gain.

You are willing to push through. This fire, this pressure, this frustration that you feel will forge you into a weapon that can battle any foe. Those who take the easy path will find themselves woefully unprepared. Not you.

To live life is a privilege, but to live it to the fullest is a choice. Pursue what you are so passionate about that you don't want to stop doing it. Be present in everything that you do. The world needs your special gift—that only you have—no matter where you are in life or what obstacles you are working through.

CHAPTER 7: ORTHODONTICS

Timeline
Chapter 7

2010

Over Memorial Day Weekend, my friend Nathan flew out from Texas to join me on the drive to San Antonio.

In June, my two-year TORP training began.

2012

In January, over Martin Luther King weekend, I competed in and won Ms. Texas United States 2012.

From January until my written board exams in April, I studied every morning at 4:30 am.

In May, my classmates and I found out we all passed.

On June 24, I graduated from residency as an orthodontist with a Masters in Oral Biology.

The following week, I competed in and won Ms. United States.

On July 20, I deployed with the Navy and landed in Toyko, Japan.

During Memorial Day weekend of 2010, my friend Nathan flew out from Texas to join me in San Diego for my last weekend before driving to Texas together. We had four days to drive my car to San Antonio along the I-10 that hugged the U.S.-Mexico border.

Nathan made the best car companion. We told stories, played games, listened to the radio, sang karaoke, reminisced about our time in Iraq on deployment, and took a rest break every few hours to recharge. On our first day, we made it all the way to a small town past El Paso, Texas, where we spent the night. The next day, at our 18th hour of driving, we made it to San Antonio. I couldn't believe what we saw along the way and hoped to do more road trips in the future.

Nathan had just finished an officer's course in San Antonio with the Army but needed to move up to Minnesota, so he quickly packed. I got settled in my new apartment in the medical center, where my movers arrived the following day. After posting an advertisement with the University of Texas, San Antonio (UTSA), I met my soon-to-be new roommate Kasey the following week.

Kasey and I knew instantly we were a great fit after we talked on the phone and became friends on Facebook. Funny enough we shared the name Corinne—my first name and her middle name. We also both had roots in California and were residents in school. She had just started at the Veteran Affairs Hospital program for a one-year fellowship, and I was starting my two-year orthodontic program at Lackland Air Force Base.

The first day jitters of residency were quickly replaced with stress. Like a high-speed train rolling over me, I had no idea that residency was going to kick my butt as much as it did—from week one.

The test anxiety that I thought I had put behind me in dental school hit me again. Plus there was added stress from needing to navigate three military services all under one roof; the Army, Air Force, and Navy all had their way of conducting business, so decorum, protocols, and terminology often varied. Sleep deprivation was all too familiar, but it was now on a new level I never knew existed.

During our first three weeks, we had an overall orientation that helped us understand the depth and speed we must learn over the next two years. It was like drinking water from a fire hose. I was lucky that my first assistant Stella was kind and that the lab techs Bradley and Mike were patient with me. I'm forever grateful to all three of them.

Things were stressful, but as one of the senior residents named Jake once said, "On my worst days, I remind myself that so many people would give their right arm to be here. Plus, we are getting paid more than any resident in the country."

He was right.

We all had applied, competed, and did everything we could to get here. If we ever needed a reminder of the importance of what we were working toward, we had to look no further than our patients. We were treating military members (active duty, retired, and dependents) who couldn't afford quality dental care on their own. The chance to be a role model, mentor, and healer led me to the path of becoming a dentist and eventually, an orthodontist. This is what I loved doing.

Inside the residents' room, where we each had our own small space carved out, you would feel cramped. It was the size of a broom closet, and if I pushed my chair out, I would hit one of my classmates behind me.

In my class were Diana, Joel, Breck, and Dave who were all Captains or Majors in the Army or Air Force and of the same rank as me. I was grateful for them because we would split the workload, take phone calls for each other, and help one another when we needed it. With five full-time attendees and 10 of us residents, we were constantly under the gun and grilled all the time. Lots of individual attention with a two-to-one teacher-to-student ratio but less room for error. It was great but also tough to come up for air.

I tried to remember that they pushed us because they cared about us doing well and growing, even when we didn't feel like it.

Another incredible person was my colleague and big sister in residency, Rasha. I appreciated her input and her standing up for me. For example, during my first month, I asked my program director if I could take one day of leave, vacation time to be at my friend's wedding as her bridesmaid in September. Her wedding was on a Sunday, and there were no flights available after the event to get back to Texas, so I would need Monday to travel back.

"No. And it is ridiculous you would even ask for a day off," the colonel said.

After my request was denied, I told Rasha that I was disappointed since I had just gotten back from deployment but I understood. The next day the colonel walked into my office and told me he had changed his mind and said it was fine as long as I covered an extra day of being on call. I was stunned.

Later that day, I learned that Rasha had marched into the colonel's office and said, "Why is it you have no problem giving the other docs time off to go to their kid's tournaments or leave early for an important game? Just because Corinne doesn't have a family doesn't mean she should be treated differently."

She was right about not getting equal treatment. I was on call during the holidays and often expected to help out since I didn't have a family to worry about. Most of the time it didn't bother me since my classmates were team players and I adored their families. But Rasha sticking up for me reminded me that behind every strong woman is a parachute of love, compassion, and encouragement. To be courageous you have to have an army—or in my case a navy—of people holding you.

During residency, we were required to do a research project—a Master's dissertation. Our class was the first to earn a Master's degree during the program. I wanted to research something I loved and instantly thought of tapping into my pageant queen network. I proposed my idea to my research mentor Dr. Marsh, and he loved it. My thesis would be on "A Challenge to Classical Facial Proportionality Studies: Conventional Profile and 3D Photography Versus Silhouettes."

Despite a challenging institutional review board that was required for all research to be done on human subjects, I was approved. I recruited 30 women who met my research criteria and, with their permission, took photographs of them: profile silhouettes in black and white, in color, and as a 3D image. The majority of them were pageant competitors.

I then showed the photos in random order to groups of orthodontists, oral surgeons, and laypeople two weeks apart. The results showed that oral surgeons were the most critical of facial attractiveness yet the most kind when they saw the whole 3D image. The orthodontists and laypeople rated the attractiveness of the silhouettes and profile pictures similarly, and both rated the 3D images as most pleasing.

This research mattered because orthodontists and oral surgeons play a deciding role in determining the esthetic destiny of a patient's face. However, they must take into account the patient's perception of their own face before treatment planning. Orthodontists need to study facial beauty, balance, harmony, and proportion as perceived by the general public, not just their own. Harmony and facial balance are not fixed concepts.

In fact, facial proportions are just one of many characteristics to describe facial harmony, including the convexity of the face, the prominence of the lips, the distance of upper lips from the S-line, and whether or not they had orthodontic treatment.

Everyone admires beauty, and it is truly a unique balance in nature. Beauty may be in the eye of the beholder, but to some extent, it lies in the hands of the orthodontist and oral surgeon.

It felt incredible to combine my two passions, and I was grateful to Dr. Marsh who supported my entering a pageant to recruit women. These women were pivotal in helping me earn a Master's degree in Oral Biology upon completion of my program.

In my final year of residency, I saw an opportunity to compete in a state pageant in the Texas United States System. Pageantry had been an outlet for me that gave me additional focus, discipline, and purpose. It was also a welcomed distraction from the grueling academic nature of residency.

So, in January 2012, over Martin Luther King weekend, I competed in and won the title Ms. Texas United States 2012. I was beyond excited since I was living in a state that regarded pageantry on the same level as church and football.

With Nationals set for the fourth of July, just one week after I would complete my residency program, I knew I had a lot of work to do. The first hurdle was my written boards in April. I was never good at cramming for tests, so I committed to waking up an hour early and going to work to get in an hour of studying before the day was in full swing. That way it wasn't hanging over my head, and I studied when I was the freshest to absorb the material. From January 1 until my boards in April, I woke up at 4:30 am. After four months of this, I racked up over one hundred hours of studying, and I took my boards.

In May, my classmates and I found out that we all had passed. I was elated. Consistency over time paid off. Next up was pageant preparation. This was my break from residency and a place where I could recharge. My morning routine switched from studying for the exam to hitting the gym. I couldn't believe how much better I felt starting my day this way and knew I needed to keep this up.

Before I knew it, June 24th came: the day of graduation. Admiral Elaine Wagner, the highest-ranking officer in the Navy Dental Corps, was in attendance, and I was lucky enough to be the first to go across the stage. My family arrived in their Navy Summer White Uniforms—the ones you see everyone wear in the movies or when ships arrive in port. They are sharp, pristine, and unlike any other uniform in the armed services. My family walked in like they were in a parade. You would never see something like that on an Air Force Base, but they were welcomed with awe.

I was on cloud nine. I had done it! I was an orthodontist. My 11 years of school had paid off.

The following week, I flew to Washington DC to compete at the United States Pageant system with my fellow sister Texas queens, each of us representing Junior Teen, Teen, Miss, and Ms. divisions. It felt great to let my hair down and know that residency was done. It was a fun-filled week of competing, sightseeing, and bonding.

One week after the pageant, my Texas State Director, Heather, called me. I had been crowned Ms. United States but was leaving soon. The Navy had an assignment for me, and I was leaving for Japan in two weeks.

The news of deployment was both exciting but also disappointing. I had just won my first national title in the big leagues and wouldn't be able to enjoy it in the states, nor would I get to participate in all the activities the national director had planned.

But, my job in the Navy came first. In some ways, I was saying goodbye to a chapter of my life. And moving is never easy. I began to get my affairs in order and promised to come back to Texas in October to crown my successor.

(2019 American Association of Orthodontists Conference in Los Angeles, California.)

Advice

In my journey to become an orthodontist, I traveled a winding path. Although I initially thought I'd go into pediatrics, I had people and events come into my life that steered me on a new course. Being open to new paths, directions, and courses should be encouraged in everyone, especially children.

As you dive into your goals, you can always adjust. Sometimes you may feel like you are moving away from them but celebrate the learning no matter where it takes you. A different view and a new perspective are great things.

A true leader takes their team to places that they can't go alone. The easy route to anything great and fulfilling in life never pays well. The only route that does is the hard one, whether that's in school, at the gym, in your career, or in life.

People who do things consistently and on time will surpass the people who are naturally talented and gifted. Believe in yourself, be headstrong, stay mentally tough, and know that you will fail more often than you succeed, but it's what you do when you fall down that matters. It's in how you will get back up. There may be someone out there who is stronger, quicker, and younger but there is no excuse not to be the hardest worker and the best version of you.

Are you interested or are you committed? If you are interested, you will let excuses and obstacles in your life take over. However, if you are committed, you will put in the work and figure out a way to make it happen.

Step 1: Set a goal.
Step 2: Make a commitment to achieve it.
Step 3: Figure out how you are going to do it.

Love the truth about yourself. It's better to fail spectacularly than to skate by and do something mediocre. If you love what you're doing, persistence will pay off. It doesn't matter how long it takes. When you want to give up, don't, you've got to be relentless. The harder the battle, the sweeter the victory.

Seeing what you become in the process is more important than the dream. The kind of person you become, the character you build, the courage you develop, and the faith manifest are what matter. You become a different kind of person and walk with a different kind of spirit. And the people who know what life is will see that you embraced it. You know it's hard and you did it anyway.

Tough times never last, but tough people do.

CHAPTER 8: MOTIVATIONAL SPEAKER

Timeline
Chapter 8

2012 In July, I deployed with the Navy to Japan.

As Ms. United States 2012, I spoke at churches, visited local hospitals, and worked closely with the public affairs officer to find meaningful ways to fulfill the duties of my crown as best I could.

2013 In the Spring, I spoke at a STEM Conference on base in Yokosuka coordinated by the Department of Defense. I was keynote speaker for 1,000 middle school girls.

I also spoke to groups on base (raising money for local auctions), at Friendship Day with the Girl Scouts, and even at birthday parties for kids coping with one of their parents being away on deployment.

In August, I won the title Ms. Galaxy 2014.

2014 In the Fall, the Navy sent me back to San Diego.

2015 I began hosting the Navy's pediatric and orthodontics continuing education leadership courses each February to recruit other speakers.

I chaired the Navy Dental Corps Birthday Ball in August.

2017 In June, I received orders to deploy to Italy in July.

My speaking event in Italy was at a press conference where other officers and I judged a fashion show.

A week later, I had the honor of modeling in a fashion show exhibition that brought awareness to breast cancer, rape victims, and natural disasters in Sicily -- while wearing couture by Miriana Spinello.

2018

After winning Ms. Earth 2018, I launched a highway cleanup project and then flew to Morocco to teach English, perform dental exams, and volunteer my time for over 100 children and teachers in Azrou.

2020

In March, COVID-19 shut everything down.

By July, I had spoken at over 20 events in Italy and throughout Europe.

In September, I left Italy to return to Japan.

By April of 2013, I had done appearances as Ms. United States 2012 for eight months while on leave and during liberty time.

I did a lot of the reachout myself, so I had to find balance in juggling my job as a naval officer and my duties as Ms. United States. I spoke at churches, visited local hospitals off base, and worked closely with Public Affairs Officer Richard McManus. Time management was key, so I got up early to work out and beat the traffic to base and schedule appearances for after working hours.

Every step of the way, I made sure my boss and the people I worked with knew what my plans were. Everyone was supportive. Life in the military, especially overseas, can get quite lonely so I found getting involved both on and off base was the best way to get plugged in and give back.

Springtime in Japan not only brought cherry blossoms but also a Science Technology Engineering and Mathematics (STEM) Conference to my base in Yokosuka, Japan. One day an event coordinator from the Department of Defense Education Activity (DoDEA) school came to my office to ask me to speak at their upcoming STEM day.

I said yes immediately and was honored when they asked me to be the keynote speaker. Yet, I quickly became nervous when I realized it was going to be for 1,000 middle school girls.

How was I going to keep their attention for 25 minutes, let alone five? I needed to be relatable and approachable. I needed to erase any misconceptions they may have formed about beauty queens or military leaders. As I began writing my speech, I thought back to when I was a little girl growing up on these military bases and what it felt like to be the new kid in school year after year, wear glasses, be petite, and feel like everyone else was pretty but me.

So, I laid it all out. I shared all my childhood memories that showed the vulnerable sides to me. I wanted every girl who was self-conscious in the back of the room to hear me. I wanted any girl who hated wearing her glasses because she was called four eyes to feel seen. I wanted the girl who felt like she didn't belong to feel that she wasn't alone.

I wanted the girls to see that the woman they saw looking perfect in a crown and military uniform was just like them. Sometimes people only see a book cover and not what's inside. My speech intended to pull back the curtain and show realness. Vulnerability is emotional bravery.

So, I showed them who I really was and what sacrifices I had made along the way to get where I am today. For 25 minutes the room was silent. My hands were sweaty holding on to my index cards that I used as a guide in case I forgot my talk.

Did you know that public speaking is most people's greatest fear? For me it was, and I remember practicing for weeks before this talk, making sure I slowed down, pronounced my words clearly, and memorized as much as I could of what I had to say.

I spoke to these girls as if they were my close friends because I wanted them to see that when it comes to feeling fear with public speaking, getting bullied, moving a lot as a military kid, or feeling crippling test anxiety, I knew the emotional turmoil all too well.

Sometimes we must break the pattern before the pattern breaks us. Cycles exist because they are excruciating to break. It takes an astronomical amount of pain and courage to disrupt a familiar pattern. Sometimes it seems easier to keep running in the same circles, rather than facing the fear of jumping and not possibly landing on your feet.

I shared with them my story of who I was, but not just of the woman wearing a crown and sash. Here are a few highlights I tried to impart to them:
- Your future is yet to be written.
- The seconds that pass are ours for the taking—we can turn them into moments that last forever.
- True love is rare, true friendship is even rarer, so make sure to cherish the friendships you have.
- When it comes to goals and dreams, you have to put in real effort. Effort means you care about something. It means it's important to you and you're willing to work toward it.
- However, a goal without a plan is just a wish.

- Be comfortable in your own skin. Find out what makes you happy and what makes you glow, then own it.
- How you love yourself is how you teach others to love you.
- It's not about lifting heavy objects or having a certain physique that makes you strong, it's your ability to overcome and do things that you once thought you couldn't do.
- Struggles develop strength.
- When life gets tough, throw down and buckle up because life is tough and so are you.

I finished and the crowd erupted with the girls rushing to the stage to take a photo with me. I had given my first motivational talk and felt an immediate adrenaline rush. I knew I had shown them vulnerability, authenticity, and genuineness confidently. Some of them walked up to me in tears and told me they were glad they were not alone and could share in my struggles. I wanted these girls to know to never stop dreaming. When you want something, all the universe conspires to help you achieve it. Have the courage to follow your dream. I told them, "I'm not here to be average, I am here to be awesome. Go confidently in the direction of your dreams. Live the life you've imagined."

After many photos, I interviewed on the Armed Forces Network (AFN) – a television broadcast only in military bases overseas and rushed back to the hospital to change into my scrubs. For the remainder of the day, groups of these girls would be rotating through various stations on base to see the careers in science, technology, engineering, and mathematics they could have if pursuing a higher level of education in this concentration.

Fellow dentists and I had them bend wire and take impressions of their hands. When the girls first saw me in scrubs, they didn't believe it was me. I now looked far different than the girl with a crown on her head on stage. But they quickly realized that none of us have to be boxed into one category. We can do it all.

My public speaking grew in Japan to include groups on base who were raising money for local auctions and even birthday parties where kids were coping with having one of their parents away on deployment. I knew how they felt since I had experienced it all too well myself. There were times when I would forget what I was going to say and have to wing it or simply laugh it off and acknowledge I was human. I found I was more critical of myself and the mistakes I made than anyone else was. It's funny how we notice our weaknesses more than the people around us.

After my time with the United States pageant concluded, I decided to compete internationally for the first time for the Galaxy pageant. Pageants are not as revered in Asia as they are in the United States. But if there was one thing I found universal between the Japanese and US in addition to smiling it was a love for anything that sparkled. They were obsessed with my crown and the diamonds on my sash. They all kept asking to try it on. Of course I said yes because their enthusiasm was infectious.

That year, in 2013, I trained hard and curtailed my Asian lifestyle to match the needs of the pageant (e.g. cutting back on my favorite foods packed with sodium and carbs like ramen, shabu shabu, baked goods, and sweets). And when it came time to compete, I won, and was named Ms. Galaxy 2014 (this one had you serve the year following the competition).

In August, upon returning to Japan after the competition, I hit the ground running to make the biggest impact I could right away. My first large-scale main event was Friendship Day with the Girl Scouts. The first time they had held the event in years with both American and Japanese Girl Scouts, it was humbling to watch hundreds of girls who didn't share a language still find ways to communicate. Each girl wanted to say so much to her foreign counterpart but was nervous about offending. Respect, manners, and etiquette were on everyone's minds as lifelong friends were made. I think we all felt nervous and excited that day.

Another event I was proud to be part of was the biannual Persian rug auction. I never had formal auctioneer training but loved the fast-paced talking, adrenaline in the room, and energy of the crowd. That night we raised $20,000 for scholarships to be given to high school seniors on base.

After the military transitioned me to the States in the Fall of 2014, I found myself hosting the Navy pediatric and orthodontics continuing education course each February where I recruited speakers. There I ironed out the technical details such as microphone and sound tests, ensuring slide compatibility, and other small but vital parts in speech preparation. These fine technological details could make or break someone's speech.

During this time, I also mentored three women into Navy orthodontics and joined the Junior League where I became a rising leader. In August 2015, I was also the chair of the Navy Dental Corps Birthday Ball in San Diego for which I set a record number of attendees.

Later, in June 2017, the military relocated me to Italy with just two week's notice. I sold my car to CarMax the night before deployment and had a friend drive me to the airport. The next morning, I woke up in a new country and a new world. I felt like a fish out of water in Sicily, but knew speaking the language and plugging myself into the community was the fastest way to be immersed and make an impact.

Like Japan, Italy had a robust public affairs office with both military and civilian contacts. It was here I met Dr. Alberto Lunetta who had an impressive number of events lined up for me as well as great connections in the community. My first time speaking was at a press conference where other officers and I judged a fashion show for which the winner won a year-long internship with a famous Italian designer.

The following week, I stood backstage before the show of another event and the Director of the Beauty and Art Academy, Liliana Nigro, walked up to me with a tape measure and began speaking Sicilian at a rapid speed with Dr. Lunetta. The next thing I knew I was being undressed and put into a red lace gown with taffeta and tulle that trailed behind me as far as the eye could see. I tried telling her that I was twice the age of the models in the show, but she kept saying, "Va bene." That was Italian for, "It's all good."

All our dreams come true if we have the courage to pursue them. Ever since I was a little girl, I wanted to model but at 5'3" my dream changed to just attending a fashion show and sitting in the audience. Fast forward 20 years later to this moment, and I was asked to wear an Italian couture dress by Miriana Spinello on the eve of the St. Agatha Celebration. I had the honor of modeling in a fashion show exhibition that brings awareness to breast cancer, rape victims, and natural disasters in Sicily. My dream of modeling came true that night.

After that incredible event, I shared what I did in Japan with Dr. Lunetta and told him I wanted to not only speak but also learn Italian so I could speak off base too. Over the next three years, Dr. Lunetta had me speak at over 20 events.

Initially we did International Women's Day where I met with women in the Italian military, police, and prison systems. From there it bridged to local Lions Clubs, professional community meetings, and schools from middle school to university.

Speaking in Italy was very different than in Japan and the US because I needed to pause often to allow for translation. As a naturally fast speaker, I had to make a conscious effort to slow down so much that it was uncomfortable for me. However, it forced me to be clearer in my pronunciation and allow for the occasional Italian words to come in that I had practiced. I never became fluent, so I spoke English when on stage, but was able to get by day to day with my Italian skills.

The variety of walks of life I met were remarkable. In Italy, the schools focus more on certain areas in the late adolescent years. For example, the schools I spoke to where they were teenagers would focus on language, music, hospitality, or cosmetology. Learning how to speak and inspire these kids with my own story was sometimes tricky since I wasn't sure if the translated version would come across the way I intended. Since a picture is worth a thousand words, I knew sharing a slideshow and videos would add validation and provide leverage to bridge my message.

At the end of every talk, I took photos with those who wanted to, answered questions, and offered my social media contact info. I admired what these kids were going through and, although in some ways we were a world apart, I prayed the glimpses of hope I shared would give them the courage they needed to do what they wanted to do in their lives. No barrier could stop my intention to make a positive impact.

In my first few months in Italy, I became intensely aware of my environment. I noticed the trash, graffiti, and wear and tear on the buildings. Sicily had an old world charm which I loved but I was saddened at how it was neglected. I wanted to help.

One great thing about Europe as a whole is its focus on the environment. I was living on the largest island in the Mediterranean and with that came a personal responsibility to preserve it. So I competed for Ms. Earth in 2018 knowing an international title could allow me to focus on giving back more in Sicily. After I won, I vowed to do several projects to clean up, improve upon what previous titleholders had done, and plant the seed of determination in the youth. Some title holders let their crown and banner sit on a shelf collecting dust. Not me. I rolled up my sleeves and got to work.

My first project involved a partnership with the United Nations Educational, Scientific, and Cultural Organization (UNESCO) and Taormina Lion's Club where we cleaned up the highway road that connected the autostrade to the city. It was the main access road and heavily trafficked.

Next, I flew to Morocco to teach English, perform dental exams, and volunteer my time for over 100 children and teachers in Azrou. This trip was very hard to coordinate with my military duties, but it was important to me, so I took vacation time and paid for the trip out of pocket.

My public speaking skills were put to the test since I didn't speak Arabic or French and, as a Westerner, had completely opposite cultural norms and mannerisms. For example, outside of the school I was told not to make eye contact with, say hello to, or smile at people, especially men, because it was seen as a form of flirtation. We also had to stop completely and fall silent during calls for prayer. For clothing, I was instructed to dress in oversized clothes without a lot of color. And, lastly, I couldn't leave the confines of the home without a bodyguard.

I learned very quickly, however, that when you speak to a group some things are universal: a smile, a song, a picture, joining hands, and taking a photo to show gratitude. During my lessons, I created crafty exercises for the kids to learn better by tapping into each one of their senses and keeping them engaged. They turned tongue blades for my dental exams into stick figure families, buttons into turtles, and shredded paper and cotton balls into rainbows. A lot of the crafts were recycled supplies and items I found searching around the house. I learned that to become a good speaker you must know your audience and find ways to connect with them and get them engaged.

My introductions were in their native languages and then we switched to forms where the kids could be actively involved. For example, the day we learned about colors, we said them in all three languages, made a rainbow on each of their desks, and sang a song about colors about not only what they look like but how they feel. That's the beauty of speaking—you learn from your audience.

For me, the three to five-year-old kids showed me that when you let go of who you are, you open yourself to become someone new and in that journey you become part of their culture. It didn't matter where I came from, what I looked like, or the fact I was battling a stomach cold. What mattered was that I was there. Their enthusiasm, desire to learn, and craving just to be acknowledged made all the stresses of my trip fall away. I was there for them and they were for me. As I spoke the few words I learned in their native language, I felt stronger and more resilient. I felt like I could walk a little bit in their shoes to experience what their world was like. No heat, no paved roads, regular electricity shortages—but a spirit, passion, and purpose stronger than any fears I had.

I was humbled how quickly the children learned despite the cultural and language difference. You must create space in your mind to allow someone to come in and by keeping your heart and mind open you allow the side of confidence and vulnerability to come through. A conscious mind can only think of one thing at a time, so if you're thinking of something helpful you cannot think of something hurtful at the same time.

This journey continued for me after I left Morocco and in my successive pageants. Sometimes my audience was just two people, sometimes it was 200. The ages varied significantly. Lessons I learned were to know your material through and through and be able to explain in a multitude of ways, practice in your environment, don't wear something that is distracting to you since it will distract the audience and be confident, you got this.

Where you started is not where you finished. Your presence is not your potential for this task but who you need to become because that needs to be your focus. Speak to inspire not to impress. Be so good they can't ignore you. I've learned the road to success is always under construction so chase your purpose and success will follow you.

Never underestimate the power of your influence.

I'm a gladiator, a unicorn, a change agent that needs to lead and know that it will cost me everything because I need to speak for those who don't have a voice or know how to use it. My superheroes are the kids I met on base, my patients, and corpsmen I met who have big dreams that just need to be reminded they can handle any situation, obstacle, or barrier they encounter.

(2012 STEM Conference Sponsored by the DODEA at Commander Fleet Activities Yokosuka, Japan)

Advice

I've learned that, as Maya Angelou has famously said, people forget what you said and forget what you did, but they will never forget how you made them feel. Life is full of stories and your ability to communicate it humanizes you. With each story comes experiences and memories and I was excited to see where it goes.

Live a life that will outlive you.

If we don't educate our youth, none of the changes we make today will carry on tomorrow. For example, think of our planet. It is the only thing that all seven continents, 193 countries, and countless cultures have in common.

Success is not measured on the days when the sun shines. Success is measured on the dark, stormy, and cloudy days. There will be bad days, there will be dark days, but you have to embrace them all. Pain is what makes you stronger. You will never understand what you went through until you see the strength, the power, the perseverance, and the resilience inside you revealed through obstacles. If you can't absorb failure, you will never meet success.

You have to believe that a new dawn follows a dark night. Your weaknesses will become strengths, your confusion will become clarity, your anxiety will become peace. Better things are coming for your life.

Lessons I learned through motivational speaking was to plan ahead and network. My journey started years ago by looking at where in my life I could improve and change for the better. I took the skills that motivated me in pageantry and applied them to all areas of life.

I was not naturally good at everything that I tried. Far from it. But I put in time, effort, and patience to learn how to cook, how to work out smarter, and how to apply stage makeup. These things and others required planning and building a team who could help bring out the best in me.

We all have gifts and a message to share with the world. When you become very good at doing what you say, the impact of your message will increase.

Engage in personal growth. Learn how to empower yourself. The moment you stop learning, your mindset becomes old and outdated.

Be humble, you don't know everything but where you will be in six months, 18 months, or 10 years from now is far better than where you are today.

To become the 1%, you've got to do what the 99% won't do. If you get in the habit of being mediocre, it becomes a part of your consciousness. If you get in the habit of giving less than you take, it will become foundational in your personality. It will damage your psychology. To counteract that, you will need to reset new, higher standards for yourself.

Tell yourself, "I'm going to harness my will and learn how to tune out the critics outside and inside me."

Take the negativity, those feelings of unworthiness, and the belief that you're not good enough and then put them in a box and ship them out of your life.

Often, you must give up something to get something.

There is greatness in you.

You must fail 100 times to succeed once. You only learn when you fail. The greatest people who have ever walked this earth have all failed at things but they learned to use failures as a tool. It's a powerful tool. Only when you apply what you have learned from trying and failing can you succeed—that is how winning is done.

CHAPTER 9: LIVING OVERSEAS IN JAPAN—PART 1

Timeline
Chapter 9

2012

On July 20th, I landed in Tokyo and began working in the Navy clinic the following Monday.

Every six weeks, I flew to Nagasaki to see patients at US Fleet Activities Sasebo.

2013

In January, I went to Sapporo, the capital of Hokkaido in Japan.

In April, I traveled to Cambodia.

That summer, I connected with Jeff and Vanessa and started taking fun adventure travel trips with girlfriends.

2014

In October, the Navy sent me back to San Diego.

I spent Christmas with family for the first time in over four years.

I joined the Junior League of San Diego and threw myself into giving back and networking with new people.

2017

In July, I was deployed to Sicily, Italy.

On July 20, 2012, I landed in Tokyo, Japan. Inhabited by over 30 million people, Tokyo is larger than New York City but also incredibly clean and organized. I marveled at the new world I saw around me – a fish out of water in a new country on a new base. My only possessions were what fit in my suitcase.

At the pick-up bus outside the Narita airport, I met my sponsor and learned a bit about life in Japan and being an orthodontist here. I was excited to hear that I would learn and be challenged by the wide variety of dental cases.

At the clinic the following Monday, I met the team I'd be working with. Everyone in the clinic got along great, including the master labor contracts (the Japanese workers) who brought an extra feeling of harmony to the office.

Junko, Chi, Minako, and Yoriko made me feel safe and even called me "sensei," which means doctor or teacher. I was incredibly touched by their kindness, generosity, and patience. Every day I learned something new from them both in orthodontics and about Japanese culture. The majority of our patients had one American parent and one Japanese parent. As a result, the children spoke two languages and I quickly switched from "Good Morning" to "おはようございます(Ohayōgozaimasu)."

During my 26-month tour in Japan, I flew down to Nagasaki every six weeks to see patients at U.S. Fleet Activities Sasebo, another Naval Base that was part of my command. I remember boarding the flight singing Lady Gaga to myself. The Japanese move, travel, and do everything quickly and quietly, so I soon realized that I was a stereotypical loud American. With what felt like a million eyes rested upon me, I hastily took off my headphones, met their gaze, said I'm sorry ごめんなさい (Gomen'nasai), and bowed— something incredibly common in Japan to show respect to others.

The flight attendants became very familiar with me since I took the same flight every six weeks like clockwork. When you travel in Japan, you find that the seats are smaller and so is the suitcase allowance size. I learned to pack minimally, saving space and weight for my orthodontic cases and instruments. With so much travel, I came to see, love, and admire the customer service exhibited at every level and stage of travel. On every flight, the attendant laid a blanket on me while I slept and made sure I had a cup of green tea waiting for me when I woke up. Service like this in an economy seat was never something I saw in the U.S.

Many people asked me what it is like to live in Japan and what I loved most. I loved being tall here. As a 5'3" American, I was the same height or taller than most Japanese. I also basked in the safety and cleanliness everywhere I went. The sushi was unbelievable. And the kindness of the people was moving.

They do a lot of things opposite in Japan like drive on the other side of the road, dial 119 for emergencies, and work in small spaces, but they were incredibly accommodating to me and other Americans. I met many expats—called Gaijin (外人) which means "outsider" or "alien"—who had a Japanese spouse or were on a work visa and truly had embraced the Japanese culture.

The strength of the camaraderie I felt overseas from my fellow dental officers was equal to what I felt on deployment. Camaraderie overseas seemed stronger than stateside because we were cut off from support systems and had only each other to get through any obstacles that arose in a foreign land. This was especially true for those of us who lived off base. I was lucky to meet several Americans in my condo building and spent a lot of time with one woman whose husband was deployed. A dual military couple living above me – Lesley and BJ – also invited me over many times. We even shared rides since we both drove beat-up cars that broke down often.

In Japan, everyone followed the rules without question. Punishment for crimes was so severe that few people committed them. Traveling to other countries in Asia quickly reminded me how living in Japan was like living in "the Switzerland of Asia," and it made me even more grateful for my life in my new home.

During my over two-year stay, I had several people come to visit and I loved exposing them to the arts, festivals, parks, and seasonal landscapes. With my friend Carlie and my cousins Robert and Victor Paul, we dressed up as geishas in Kyoto. With my friend

Jacqueline and my brother Nick we walked through cherry blossoms, known as Sakura, that looked like snow decorating the streets. With my friends Chelsea and Kristen we marveled at the brilliant colors of autumn I never knew existed.

With a new base came new friends. During my first week in orientation, I met Vivienne. She was a judge advocate general (JAG), which is a Navy lawyer. She was also very new to the Navy, and we quickly bonded over our love for our careers, travel, Kate Spade, and seeing the world as a big adventure. Through her, I met several other lawyers and their spouses, many of whom became life-long friends.

I found that living in the greater Tokyo area meant harsh winters with several big snowstorms. But with close access to a big airport, I made sure to plan a trip somewhere warm during every holiday. I went to explore Singapore, Vietnam, Cambodia, Korea, Taiwan, Malaysia, and Thailand. Since most American holidays we got off were just regular days of the week for the locals, the cost of getaway trips was irresistible. Each year, I got to visit about seven to nine countries and experience worlds I had never dreamed of.

During my first winter—and birthday month of February—I went to Sapporo, the capital of Hokkaido in Japan to connect with my friend June who I had met through a colleague. Over the next few days, I learned she was the epitome of the traveler extraordinaire. She shared my love for travel as well as fashion, friendship, exploration, and positivity for life. We even had a similar military upbringing. We quickly bonded and when she invited me to come to Cambodia and Thailand with her friends, I said yes.

So in April 2013, I boarded a flight for Phnom Penh, the capital of Cambodia. As I exited the airport, I saw a dirt road and a world turned back in time. Then suddenly, it felt like a million people were trying to get my attention all at once. My anxiety quickly spiked when I almost agreed to get in a car with the wrong driver.

No one spoke English, and I was traveling alone. Luckily, I did find the correct driver, and we headed to the hotel. June, her husband, and the rest of the crew met up with me the next morning. We started our adventure of exploring the city in our tuk-tuk—a small taxi with no doors. It's like a fast golf cart that drives into oncoming traffic. As we made our way to our tour guide, I became fascinated with this new land. I had never heard of the Killing Fields, nor did I know much of the history of Cambodia, but I was shocked and humbled to hear what happened not that long ago.

More than a million people were killed and buried by the Khmer Rouge regime (the Communist Party of Kampuchea) during its rule of the country from 1975 to 1979. This holocaust was not limited to race, religion, or economic status—instead, if you were educated, literate, intelligent, or spoke another language besides Khmer (Cambodia's national language), then you were a target because you were seen as a threat to the dictators. People were starved and taken out to fields to work until they collapsed. The former leaders of the Khmer Rouge who had committed these crimes and some of the political leaders who supported them were still alive.

While there, I walked around the graves of those men, women, and children who were tortured and buried. One area had colored yarn tied around a small fence area—this was where the baby and toddler graves rested. I gasped at the sight of everything and held back my tears. How did I not know about this?

The final site I saw was a small square-shaped fortress several stories high with clear panels. When I walked closer I saw it was full of bones of skulls, ribs, femurs, toes, and every other bone you can name. My heart sank to think of the atrocities this country had gone through and how this horrific past was not that distant. What I saw and learned are things I will never forget.

After exploring Phnom Penh, we went to Siem Reap, home of Angkor Wat. This holy ground consisted of temples that were thousands of years old. Even though it was April, it was incredibly hot and humid. Trying to be respectful of the religious spaces, we wore long sleeves and all sweated through our clothes.

I was surprised that this Hindu temple wasn't listed as one of the Seven Wonders of the World. I had been to the Great Wall of China, the Colosseum in Rome, and knew I would hike Machu Picchu in Peru. Each of these places is magnificent and has an intense purpose and impact. Angkor Wat exhibited each one of these traits with equally intense magnitude. While at Angkor Wat, we saw monks and were told not to touch them but that we could pray with them. I felt like I was in a Lara Croft movie, except this was real life and I hoped the dangers she encountered weren't lurking around every corner.

Back at our hotel, we enjoyed the comfort of cooling off in the pool and taking naps during the heat of the day before heading to the markets in the evening. We couldn't get over how cheap everything was. It was 50 cents for a taxi ride and $10 for an hour-long massage by the pool. It reminded me how lucky we all were to have good jobs and be able to do trips like this.

During lunch one day, I asked June if she would come with me to pick up something at the store. I needed a new razor. We told our group where we were going and walked across the street to what I thought was a store. Inside, the gentlemen at the counter held up a clear bag with a hundred razors. I shook my head, thinking I'd need a tetanus shot after just looking at the bag, and quickly made my way to another store where I found an individually packaged razor. While I was making the purchase, June noticed a small crowd of men began to form around us.

I grabbed June's hand, leaving my change on the counter, and we ran back across the street. As petite women, we were a potential target for begging, theft, or worse. I realized it wasn't safe to venture out alone like that without one of the men in our group. It was the first time I fully felt what it is like to be a foreigner and a minority (a valuable experience for all of us, actually).

I also learned it's smart to be aware of your environment and not let complacency set in. There is safety in numbers, so it's best not to travel alone. Being with a group of friends you trust is priceless.

All this being said, it wasn't often that I felt scared or nervous in Cambodia. More often than not I was extremely touched by the kindness shown by people in this country.

After three days in Siem Reap, we left and made our journey to Thailand. Many people don't know but Thailand means "land of the free" in Thai. Their country has its shape due to the treaties and negotiations done over the years with the various kings to ensure they could maintain the sovereignty of their nation.

The weather was warm and humid, and the cuisine was hot and spicy. We marveled at the colors and flavors in the food and drink. Again it felt like we entered into a whole new world that we never knew existed. We spent a few days in Chiang Mai, making our way to various temples where we paid our respects and prayed for kindness, wealth, and happiness in our lives.

Despite the record-high temperatures and humidity, we were also required to dress conservatively when we visited these temples. A sign of affluence was fair skin, so many people wore puffy jackets with fur-lined hoodies that completely covered their faces and heads to avoid getting a tan.

Shoulders, arms, and legs had to be covered when entering these holy grounds, so we sweated through all our clothes and had to wash them daily so we didn't smell. While in Thailand, we had the opportunity to ride on elephants, lay with tigers, and hold snakes (something I'm deathly scared of). The snake was blind and safe to hold, so I partnered up with Jackie (who was also just as scared), and we decided to go for it since we knew this was a once-in-a-lifetime opportunity to face our fears head-on. I held the middle portion and tail, she held the head. As they draped the huge snake over our shoulders, we did our best not to shake. I just kept telling myself to breathe and smile. Take the photos fast!

Note: Our tour guides made sure that we went to areas where the animals were treated well and had been rescued from abuse.

This amazing trip further ignited my travel bug and made me ready for more. And each trip that followed inspired me to explore off the beaten path further and further.

During my second summer there in 2013, I connected with a couple named Jeff and Vanessa. Jeff was a lawyer with the same rank as me, and Vanessa was this brilliant, beautiful blonde finishing up her PH.D. It felt great to meet a couple who I had so much in common with and admired deeply. Since Jeff was pulled in many directions for his job and traveled back and forth to the states, Vanessa and I planned our own trips together.

Our first girls' trip was to Kuala Lumpur, the capital of Malaysia. Vanessa, two other girlfriends, and I happily left the cold winter weather in Japan over Valentine's weekend and traded it for the warm weather of Southeast Asia. As you can imagine, we four American women stood out, and we took our safety seriously. The world views Americans as the richest people in the world and when you travel it can make you a target.

One night, Vanessa and I decided to get drinks after dinner at a nearby Hyatt hotel. We were dressed up in our cocktail dresses, so we wanted to go somewhere to dance and enjoy the rooftop views. As we entered the hotel and looked for how to access the rooftop, we were greeted by staff who thought we were hookers. Yes, hookers—not two highly educated women just enjoying their Saturday night. We were disgusted but didn't let it ruin our evening, so we headed upstairs to the rooftop bar.

After we sat down, it quickly became apparent that we would not be served by the bar staff. And other guests stared at us, seemingly to ask, "Why are *you* here?"

We couldn't believe it. So, we decided to leave. We flagged down a taxi to take us to our hotel. As we got in, the driver asked, "How old are you ladies? Where are you from?"

Quickly, we knew we weren't safe.

"We are 65," we lied, more than doubling our age and hoping it would put an end to the conversation.

We got out as soon as we could. Two taxi rides later, after no drinks and no dancing, we made it back to our hotel—we had gotten a great deal at the Ritz Carlton. As much as we both wanted to let our guard down and enjoy a night out, we learned that it's nearly impossible to do so without having men with us.

The experiences we had didn't deter us from traveling but they did make us more mindful and plan more in advance. We had researched what to wear during the day at temples but did not think to research how to dress at night out on the town. Traveling in a foreign country means not just abiding by the rules and customs but also learning how to blend in respectfully. As Americans in Asia, however, it's hard not to stand out, so I've learned that having local tour guides and drivers with me at all times is key to having a safe and enjoyable experience.

Back in Japan, life in Tokyo had many perks of big city living like convenience, choice, nightlife, and tons of things to do but without the trash and crime that typically is associated with city life.

Although Tokyo is a big, modern city, many of my friends who visited had tattoos and found that they are considered taboo in Japan since they are usually associated with the Yakuza (the Japanese mafia). It was best to cover them up. This became challenging, however, when we went to an onsen—a Japanese bathhouse. Many were stand-alone structures that you could find in every town no matter the size. Most of them were separated by gender and open until the early hours of the morning. I was immediately a fan. It was the perfect place to relax and soak your feet after a long day of walking. One time, after visiting the Nikko shrine with my friends, all the Japanese women stared at us when we entered. We had more curves and less hair in certain places than they did. No one was ever rude; they were simply intrigued to see such different-looking people partake in their customary ritual.

Fashion that fit was hard for me to find since I, like many American women, had curves. I remember searching in Tokyo for an evening gown with my friend Lesley and everything we found reminded us of an 80's movie. We found puffy dresses with lace and tulle everywhere that completely swallowed us up. The colors were pastel, neon, or other hues that were out of fashion. Nothing we tried on made us feel pretty. This was where we relied on friends mailing their dresses from back home to us to help us out.

Another tough thing to find was shoes. In two years, I destroyed 14 pairs of shoes beyond repair by walking everywhere. Unlike the US where many of us drive, the Japanese rely heavily on public transportation like trains and buses. They are faster, more dependable, and produce less traffic in getting people from point A to B. But there also is a lot of walking involved without private transportation.

What I saved on fashion, I spent on self-care. The Japanese understood how daily life struggles do a number on our feet and skin, and I soon adopted the practice of wearing gloves and large hats to protect myself. I also sought out the best skincare from locals who understood American skin. I used to marvel at how the lady who did my nails was 42 years old but didn't look a day over 25. So, I started to follow her regimen: layer yourself with sunscreen anytime you go outside and reapply often, wear driving gloves (and use ones that pull up past your elbows in the summer months), and wear big hats or carry a UV umbrella. After doing this for just a little while, I could tell my skin appreciated it.

Two years flew by in Asia and my next set of orders brought me back to San Diego in October 2014. Back home, I had been away for four and a half years, and the idea of having Christmas with my family was surreal—gone were the years where I took this for granted. I missed sitting down at a large table with all the family, my Aunt Barbara's sticky buns, and opening up presents around the tree together. After dinner it was always about the games, where my family would get so competitive they would make up words or try to find ways to bend the rules. Our phones had to be put away, and time would stand still as we shared stories and a lot of laughter.

But aside from holiday fun with family, I definitely went through reverse culture shock as buying a car and finding a place to live took over my world. Starting over again was harder than expected.

Moving back meant a new chapter with both familiar faces and some new ones. Many of my old friends had gotten married, started families, or moved away from San Diego while I was gone. This new tour I was starting was going to be different because I would be completing my obligation of service to the Navy (in 2015 I would have "paid back" the Navy for the residency program I completed in Texas in 2012), and could go into private practice if I choose. If I stayed in the Navy, I would be sent overseas again, which was amazing but it also meant my personal life would be put on hold. I needed to decide what I wanted next.

Each new place had plunged me into depths of uncertainty, with new people, places, languages, cultural norms, and obstacles to navigate. At times I even felt panic and anxiety well up inside of me. In the military, we sacrifice a lot of freedoms that most people take for granted. Sometimes it takes a toll on us even on our good days. We don't have the option to give up or bow down.

I have learned though that what matters more is building a growth mindset deep in your subconscious that allows you to look chaos in the face and tell fear to step aside. When people ask me what it's like to be constantly moving, I tell them to engage in the world in the way that you want it to look. Live in the moment and enjoy the journey.

And that's what I did. In my first few months moving back, I went to a meet and greet for the Junior League of San Diego, a philanthropic organization founded 100 years ago in New York City by a group of women who wanted to create long-lasting positive changes in their community and with themselves. There I met Vanessa (another one!) and Lisa, veterans in the organization with a wealth of knowledge that seemed parallel to running a fortune 500 company. The group of women who run this organization is a force not to be underestimated. They were even able to procure funding, supplies, and manpower for 40 other nonprofit organizations in the area that had lost government funding.

At my first charity event, I participated in and donated money to help foster youth who were acting out and at risk of getting stuck in the criminal justice system. It helped them build new skills and find purpose as contributing members of society. I was hooked and counted down the minutes to when I could turn in my application to officially join. In my first year as a pledge member, I was assigned to the hibiscus group located in Little Italy in downtown San Diego.

My provisional leaders, Michelle and Jackie, were fearless and inspiring. They allowed me to spread my wings into areas I never thought I could go like learning tax codes in finance and co-chairing fundraiser events. My enthusiasm and energy were welcomed to be fully utilized.

My mentor Mary was beautiful, smart, and radiated energy that was contagious. I instantly felt connected to her. In our first large group meeting where over 120 women filled the room, I ironically sat down next to two dentists. We bonded over our professions, empowering women, and love of giving back. I knew I was in the right place.

Over the next nine months, I threw myself into the meetings and contributed however I could and was soon invited to host my own fundraiser. The theme? A throwback to the 90's.

It felt good to meet so many talented, amazing women from industries outside the Navy and dentistry. To see life outside the military and dentistry—while getting to feel more connected to San Diego in ways I never thought I could—was priceless.

Flash forward to the middle of June in 2017, I received a hot fill order to leave and report to Sicily, Italy the following month. It was time for an international adventure once again.

(At Miyajima Island, Hiroshima Bay, Japan — Photo by Tana Lee Photography)

Advice

Get comfortable with being uncomfortable. Making mistakes is part of the adventure.

Get used to not knowing what is going on and learn to thrive in a foreign environment. You are capable of much more. Taking chances is the best thing you can ever do for yourself.

Make yourself the main character in your life's story, and live for things that make you happy. Go on spontaneous adventures and romanticize the mundane things in life.

Recognize where you are in life and don't take it for granted.

CHAPTER 10: LIVING OVERSEAS IN ITALY

Timeline
Chapter 10

2017 In July, I was deployed to Sicily, Italy.

2020 In March, COVID-19 shut everything down.

In September, I left Italy for a second tour in Japan.

I landed in Italy close to 11 pm on a night in July. My body didn't know what time it was since I had been traveling for the past two days straight on a series of commercial and military planes. My sponsor, Captain Watts, greeted me with a sign decorated with the Navy Dental Corps symbol, an oak leaf with an acorn on each side. He eagerly helped me with my two large suitcases, a carry-on bag, and a messenger bag.

As we left the military airport in Sigonella, we drove in the dark through what felt like cornfields. My mentor Captain Scott Curtice had prepared me for this a few weeks prior when we had dinner. He had been stationed in Sicily in the past and told me that it feels very rural yet is close to so many things. I was grateful for the endless list of suggestions and places to explore he shared.

Captain Watts swerved on the road, barely missing a lamb that was crossing. I was again in another world. We arrived at the hospital first so I could have my orders stamped, and then he showed me around. It wasn't until after half past midnight that I asked if he could take me to the Navy Lodge, my temporary home until my items arrived. I needed to rest and adjust to Italian time. I was exhausted.

The next morning, Captain Watts picked me up and walked with me to all my appointments and check-ins required at the command. For three weeks, he didn't leave my side so that he could help me avoid the mistakes that he had made along the way.

When I started base indoctrination, I met the infamous Andrea. His insatiable charm and excitement ignited my passion to explore the island. Being that it was August, a lot of things had shut down. So, I wasn't able to do many of the things people suggested simply because people in town were gone on vacation for "Ferragosto," a yearly holiday centered around Assumption Day. A time of rest that usually lasted two weeks, it was more like the entire month in Italy. Taking advantage of this opportunity, I signed up for as many morale, welfare, and recreation (MWR) tours to see the island and meet more people as I could.

One of my first trips was to the Aeolian Islands led by a tour guide named Monica. Monica spoke beautiful English, carried the confidence of a gorgeous Sicilian woman, and was incredibly gregarious. Being with her confirmed that I was in the right place.

Monica's family had joined our group of military members, families, and contractors on the hydrofoil ride over, and her son got very seasick. He wasn't the only one. It was August, hot, and crowded. Being near the only bathroom on the boat didn't help anyone in our group either. When we arrived at Lipari, Monica took us on a whirlwind tour of the island and pointed out the other Aeolian Islands we could see in the distance. The beaches at Lipari were unlike any place I had ever been—they had lots of rocks and crystal-clear water in shades of blue that I had never seen.

As we chatted over an Italian lunch, I learned Monica had taught herself English while working at her Uncle's hotel growing up. Later she worked in the housing office on base and improved her language skills even more. I immediately asked for her card, thinking she could be my housing counselor. I was so happy I met one of the key people on my base who could make Sicily feel like home.

The following week, I met with all the realtors for the Catania region that I could (including the ones I was warned not to by the military housing office) and explored every city people lived in from Belpasso on Mt. Etna to Acireale to Augusta. Sicily was full of old-world charm and knew the decision of where I would live could make or break my tour.

After checking out a lot of options, I realized that I was a city girl who loved being close to the action, the water, and the airport without too long of a commute to the base. Needing to make a decision soon, one of my friends at the Navy lodge introduced me to Gaetano. He was an Italian family man who worked on our base and enjoyed helping Americans. He drove me up to the bachelor pad of a young airman named Gregory who was leaving. I instantly fell in love with the place and knew it was home.

I could see past the empty walls and lack of storage, a common issue in European homes, with visions of building closets, enclaving the laundry room, and installing a wine fridge. Because the housing allowance varies by rank, status (as a contractor, government employee, or military), and size of your family, I knew negotiating would be crucial in securing this apartment. Before looking off base for housing, I was warned not to share my rank since every home would magically be priced to match my maximum housing allowance. When asked what I did in the military, I just said I helped people and worked at the hospital.

In Europe, homes are built very differently than in the States. They are empty rooms with no storage and no appliances. Outlets work on an entirely different voltage system. And screens for windows to keep pesky critters out, garbage disposals, carpet, walls that are easy to hang frames on, centralized air conditioning and heating, and remote-controlled garages are luxuries—not standard features.

One of the smartest things I learned from my previous sponsor in Japan was to measure all my furniture and inventory everything I had and then take pictures and measurements of places I visited to see if I could make it work. In my last overseas home, they moved all my items through a sliding glass door because they wouldn't fit out the front. In the military, moving isn't easy and when you add overseas components, the chances of missing or damaged items go up exponentially.

After some back and forth price negotiation and arranging for appliances like a fridge, washer, dryer, and transformers, I was able to secure the condo. I was ready to move in and let my Italian dream life commence.

Another thing I learned is that in Italy having a good landlord is just as, if not more, important than the place itself. So I was excited when the previous tenant shared great experiences with Salvo. In addition to being my landlord, Salvo also owned a large trucking dealership, spoke very good English, and was incredibly resourceful. He aided me in cleaning, maintaining, and repairing my home even when times were challenging. For example, the main toilet stopped working before I moved in and I ended up having to wait five weeks before someone came to fix it. But Salvo did try to fix it himself and then unplugged it for me to make sure it wouldn't leak until it was properly repaired. This long wait time is the norm for life in Sicily.

Small, fast cars with automatic transmissions (i.e. not stick-shifts) were hard to find, but I knew an automatic was what I needed to brave the Italian roads with their lack of infrastructure and erratic drivers. I had looked at over 20 cars and felt like it was impossible to find something. Then Andrea suggested "Subito," the Italian version of Craigslist.

Andrea taught me some key words in Italian, and I scoured the pages to find about 10 cars that fit what I needed. He helped me call every single one of them, and I narrowed it down to three options. The only one who ended up meeting with me was an Italian Navy pilot who spoke some English and worked on my base. He was expanding his family and needed to sell the car. After taking it to American Muscle, a local mechanic who checked it out, I agreed to purchase it.

Next came the process of denationalization, a series of paperwork and stamps to move it from an Italian to an American driver. I had to wait another four weeks to get the car despite having the cash in hand ready to go. Often in Italy, they say, "Va bene." This means, "It's fine." There is no rush, no sense of urgency. The idea that things can wait is commonly accepted. So, for over four weeks I went from one office to the next only to find them closed (when they were supposed to be open) and made appointments to get our paperwork processed only to be told to retrace my steps because someone missed a signature or some other new hoop had to be jumped through. I was so frustrated since I felt like I was always starting back at square one. It felt like I was making no progress at all.

One day, I broke down in Captain Watt's car because I wanted the freedom to drive a car so badly and I was already three months without one. With my place off base and a lack of public transportation, I began to feel even more vulnerable not having my own set of wheels. One weekend, a friend of mine let me borrow her car and told me it was time for me to drive. I was scared but knew I had to go for it. She lived up in Belpasso, and I had to figure out how to get home. Armed with Google Maps on my phone, I put in my address and drove slowly, letting everyone pass me until 45 minutes later, I made it back down the windy roads of the mountain and back home. The following week, I finally got my car.

Driving in Italy was like a personal, high-stakes video game. Absolute attention had to be given to the road at all times; you never knew who may dart in front of you or what pothole was waiting in the distance. The only time I saw other drivers exercise more caution was when it rained and the streets flooded.

I used to leave around 5 am and go to the gym before work because I found it more peaceful to hit the road early in the morning with fewer cars and less sporadic driving in the roundabouts. If you are not familiar with roundabouts, they are circular intersections where drivers travel counterclockwise around a center island. They are very common in Europe. Child car seats were not mandatory in Italy, so I often saw entire families riding on a Vespa motor scooter without helmets. I wondered if they had a closer relationship with God.

Living off base made me feel like I could truly embrace more of the everyday Italian lifestyle, while still keeping one foot in America while on base. Italian food was especially incredible. There were fruit and vegetable stands on the side of the road everywhere you went and farmer's markets almost every weekday morning. I remember biting into my first tomato there, not knowing tomatoes could taste so explosively delicious. Misshapen, of varying sizes and colors, and sprinkled with dirt, what the tomatoes lacked in presentation they made up in flavor. In Italy, there was no such thing as organic or gluten-free since everything was freshly made. Friends and family who visited from the States actually lost weight and were able to eat and enjoy everything despite having allergies. It made me wonder what we have in our American food.

As beautiful as Italy was, culture shock still crept up on me now and then. I remember feeling like I wanted to break down and cry when I would come home from a weekend trip and find that the power to my refrigerator had shut off and I had to throw out all my food. This happened often. Ironically the other circuit breakers in my house worked fine.

In Italy, there were constant power surges, and everything could not be all on at once or it would overload the circuit. Even a 2-bedroom apartment inside a large fairly new condo building was not immune.

Another time, I couldn't get my car out of my complex when the gate broke. I had to push it open, rallying the assistance of any stranger who passed by.

One of the toughest and scariest times was when I went to put a few things in my car and I took my car and garage keys down the five flights of stairs but forgot my house keys upstairs. My front door automatically locked, so I was stuck outside. In Italy you get over a dozen keys for your place—I had two front doors, each with different keys, a key to the laundry room, a key to every door in the house, a key for the garage, a key for the garage door, a key for the front door of the condo, a key for the back door of the condo, and a key for the swimming pool. My keys looked like something out of an old storybook that could break at any moment. To make matters worse, it was a Sunday when most businesses are closed and people are out with their families. I ran frantically up and down the stairs, knocking on doors to find someone who could help me. My wallet, house keys, and cell phone were all locked inside. After 30 minutes, dripping in sweat, I found a neighbor who helped open the underground garage door and the front gate to the complex.

A second set of house keys were in my office on my Naval base in Sigonella, a 30-minute drive away. I knew this was my best option. So, I drove there cautiously, trying not to let my emotions get the best of me. Upon entering a military base it's required to show identification. I had none. I told the security guard what happened and told him he could escort me to my office. Thankfully, he did, and I was grateful to find my spare keys in my desk. I never left my place again without my cell phone and all my keys—for the car, garage, and house.

The experience of living in Italy was completely opposite to my experience in Japan. In Italy, lunch and dinner started far later and went longer, oftentimes into the wee hours of the night. Showing up 30-45 minutes late was like being on time. Hugging and kissing were acceptable and encouraged.

In Japan, by contrast, everything ran on time and people even showed up early, lunch began between 11:30 am and noon and would never go past 1:30 pm. Starting at 5:30 pm, dinner was served with restaurants closing at 9 pm, and there was no hugging, just bowing to show respect and acknowledgment.

The great thing about working on a military base was getting to feel like you had a piece of Little America. You didn't have to worry about speaking the local language. You could find some goods you missed from home. You could even have things mailed to your P.O. Box with a US zip code. Of course, we didn't have all the luxuries from home like getting to choose from 20 different types of shampoos or face wash brands.

I often heard people say they missed Target, Chick-fil-A, or Starbucks. However, what you quickly realize is that in a world where things are not convenient, you spend less money. Having less storage prevents you from buying more stuff. As Americans, we love having big cars, huge houses, giant swimming pools, fully stocked pantries, and spacious walk-in closets. Yet in both Europe and Asia they instead seemed to value time, experience, and treasuring fewer items. It was a minimalist approach in some ways.

Minimalism is the key to success in European air travel too. When you fly with inexpensive airlines such as Ryanair, EasyJet, Volotea, and Wiz Air, you can buy a really cheap ticket, but that doesn't include luggage. And any luggage you are allowed to bring for an extra fee is far smaller than you'd think. You learn to pack light. An approved carry-on is equivalent to a medium-sized backpack.

Adjusting to this meant planning my outfits, forecasting the weather, and being strategic about activities. Even for a long weekend trip, no space could be spared. The shoes I wore on the plane were often the only ones I brought along. Sometimes my friends and I would wear multiple layers on our flights to bring more clothes than could fit in our bags. Some airlines required you to pick up any checked baggage, go outside the terminal, and then come back in to have your bags rechecked. This was problematic if the flight was delayed. So even for my week-long mission trip to

Morocco, I traveled only with a small carry-on bag and packed detergent so I could wash my clothes in the sink.

Vacationing in Europe is far different than living in Europe. In a hotel, you have a concierge you can call for help with anything. You are not worried about traffic, getting to work on time, or eating meals that stretch way past your bedtime. Yet living in Italy presented some interesting challenges. One example is that I never knew when my utility bills would arrive. I was grateful my landlord paid mine and I reimbursed him, but often they came months late.

I was grateful that a few of my military friends I met in Japan on my first tour were on mainland Italy. They were the perfect travel partners who understood the joy of cheap travel, creating memories, and laughing at the mishaps that could occur along the way. On one such trip, two of us used hairdryers at the same time and completely blew out the electrical circuit of the entire AirBnB home. The owner didn't seem to care. Navigating challenges faced in our adventures made our bonds stronger. During this tour, I even became a godmother twice to children whose names and upbringings were inspired and influenced by their parents' European experiences.

On vacation, you have tour guides and groups that show you where to go and guide you in the right direction. But when you live here, you live and die by Google maps. There are roads without signs. There are roads without clear lane path markings. Going with the flow of traffic is a dance. Stop signs are driven through without even a "California roll." Cutting other drivers off, breaking suddenly, and speeding are standard practices. Driving aggressively and with certainty is a must.

Gas is priced by the liter, so it was far more expensive than in the States. My car insurance was the highest I've ever paid at $1600 per year, but rightfully so because there were so many accidents. During my last year in Italy, my dental assistant's husband was rear-ended when he was entering the base, and his car was totaled.

Since the roads were poorly maintained, I went through six tires within three years. Monthly checkups at my local mechanic's shop were a necessity. I visited him so often that they became family. Lorenzo and Marcella, former Canadian citizens with Sicilian heritage, were my guardian angels in ensuring I always had a safe car to drive. They saved me on countless occasions by replacing alternators, wires, and more. I am truly indebted to their family.

That's the beauty of living overseas: you never know when you will meet your new best friend or interact with people who treat you like a daughter or son because of the struggles you face. The tight bonds forged grow quickly and are unshakeable.

In Italy, there are over a dozen different dialects, and the Sicilian dialect is so different that it is categorized as a completely different language. When I first moved there, I took language classes on base. They were free and so valuable to help me start to understand the culture. I learned that you understand a country when you understand its language. Plus, being able to speak the language, even if just a few words correctly and politely, was greatly helpful.

My Italian teacher, Eliana, told me that to learn a new language you must forget who you are. This meant that you had to let go of things you held on to—like vocabulary, grammar, and sentence structure—to speak the language correctly. She was right. The more I spoke and practiced, the better I got, and I found it was a great icebreaker when I was out and about. My friends who spoke Spanish quickly caught on since both are Romance languages.

On one trip, my friend Cindy taught me "Le capisci l'inglese?" which means "Do you understand English?" Because most Americans in Italy say, "Parla inglese?"— an informal way of asking, "Do you speak English?"— this phrase was a game-changer for my daily interactions. By using the formal construction, I showed I was trying to be respectful to everyone I encountered. I came across as more polite and endearing, especially when I asked with a smile.

Most people know Italy for its fashion. Yet couture fit quite differently on me and alterations often made things much tighter than requested. I found better luck with shoes, especially walking shoes. And those were a lifesaver in Europe, which is full of cobblestone roads and uneven walkways. Walking in high heels often felt dangerous like one night when I went to a charity gala. I had to grip the side of the wall to navigate an unpaved road in my cocktail dress and high heels. Although my shoes were comfortable on flat ground, I got blisters and, after a few near-missed falls, I understood why I rarely saw others wearing them.

Another challenge overseas is growing your network and meeting people you connect with, especially if you don't speak the same language. While the military camaraderie and network of local nationals on base allow you to build friendships at a faster pace than if you moved abroad on your own, what if what you need doesn't exist on base? For example, I had to search off base for a hairdresser, nail salon, and other services that made me feel pretty.

The only hairdressers who could speak English and were familiar with what I wanted for my hair were a few Americans who had moved to Sicily after gaining dual citizenship thanks to their Italian grandparents. I had appointments booked months in advance with them and never rescheduled out of fear that I wouldn't be able to get another appointment.

When it came to my nails, I tried every salon I could find before stumbling upon Corina, a sweet girl from Romania living with her boyfriend. Driving to her home for an appointment meant braving a windy road and praying my car would still be there after our appointment—car theft was a daily occurrence. Her skills and kindness were remarkable. She was always punctual and could finish in an hour whereas other salons ran late and would take up to two and a half hours. As I shared my great experience with her, her business grew, her English skills improved, and she was finally able to move out and leave her not-so-great boyfriend.

I was also lucky to meet Angie, a semi-retired travel agent, who helped me plan trips all over Italy and the rest of Europe. I was introduced to Angie by her husband, Giovanni, who was a regular tour guide on the base who I adored. Angie spoke the Queen's English, being born and raised in Malta, a nearby country formerly ruled by Britain. She had two sons, a dentist and a medical school student. Quickly I became like her surrogate daughter.

Through Angie, I learned how to travel smartly, how to take advantage of the low tourist seasons, and how to get the best price for things. Whenever we met up for high tea, she showed me how I could explore and enjoy another unique place in Sicily.

Our last time together before I left was enjoying tea and pastries in her kitchen after she had helped me when my car's battery died. That's the lovely thing about meeting people in Italy; once you are in their circle of trust, you are set. You just have to find a way in.

For me, I was able to connect with people through kindness, appreciation, and gratitude. I tried to be genuine and share with others. Despite the many detours I had living in Italy, it is one of the highlights of my military career, and I pray one day to return.

(Feb. 2018: Modeling Italian Fashion Couture by Miriana Spinello at the St. Agatha Celebration Runway Show in Catania, Sicily)

Advice

The Sicilians taught me to live as if you were to die tomorrow. But don't forget to learn as if you were to live forever by documenting what you do and sharing it.

Nothing is permanent unless you want it to be. You can always go home.

I have learned that God puts people in our lives and takes them out for reasons we may not know at the time. The same is true for where we move and where we go. Sicily wasn't on my mind before I went, but it turned out to be the best tour of my career.

CHAPTER 11: LIVING OVERSEAS IN JAPAN—PART 2

Timeline
Chapter 11

2020   In September, I landed in Iwakuni for a second tour in Japan.

2023   Projected end date of tour.

From 2012 to 2014, I lived in Yokosuka, Japan—30 miles south of Tokyo with a New York City feel.

In 2020, I returned to Japan to live in Iwakuni—30 miles south of Hiroshima with a countryside feel—for another tour.

Japan is the size of California with one-third the population of the US, and my tours had some similarities and some differences.

The people in Japan were very kind, polite, helpful, and respectful in both of my experiences. Many of my military patients spoke both Japanese and English, so I started learning the language and began to see why so many people love it there.

With a collectivist mentality, they believe that doing what's best for the group and society as a whole is more important than individualistic desires. Rules are never questioned but followed with the utmost obedience. This applies to everything in life, from building to school to work.

Japanese culture is about personal responsibility. They aren't afraid of catching someone else's germs, instead, they want to protect others from theirs. Caring for others is caring for oneself. Even under their masks, you see them smile and bow. A smile means the same thing in every language; it is a universal gesture of welcome and respect.

They are more environmentally conscious and recycle everything. I do mean everything. I have five different trash cans but could use up to 12 if I wanted. Each year the local cities in Japan put together a calendar for trash pick-up every weekday from 8 am to 10 am. If you have oversized items to dispose of, then you have to pay for that service.

They are always on time or even early. They bow often to show respect. Japan is probably the safest country in the world, and theft is rare. There were times that I left my wallet at the grocery store or forgot my iPhone on the train, only to return and find it right where I left it.

In Japanese culture, there is a lot of emphasis on honoring the present, being completely present with the people or tasks in front of you. Leave stress and worries at the door.

Despite their short stature, Japanese people are incredibly strong. Both times I moved into a condo with my American-sized furniture, the Japanese movers were quick, efficient, and careful in carrying it all up nine flights of stairs.

Buying a car in Japan is a breeze because both cars and roads are well-maintained. Since the Japanese don't like buying used cars, you can get one for about $3000 to $4000, half the price of what you would find in Europe and a fraction of the cost compared to the US. Like in Europe, though, the roads are narrow and often only fit one car when really they are meant for two cars.

Gas in Japan is much cheaper on base, but using public transportation is far more common. The trains run on time, and high-speed bullet trains called the Shinkansen can whisk you at 200 mph across the country in just a few hours. Flying in Asia is far more comfortable than on European budget flights, so long as you are short like me and are sure to pack headphones.

It is customary not to talk at all, or at least to keep conversations quiet, when on public transport. Talking on your cell phone or playing music is forbidden. Most people sleep, put on their makeup, or text. It was an adjustment, coming from Europe and the States, but I quickly saw how relaxing and peaceful it was.

After experiencing city life on my first tour, I was determined to make my countryside life for my second tour as glamorous as possible. I went out of my way to find all the hidden gems to eat, explore, and support local businesses. I met more Japanese people and practiced the language.

Basking in the laid-back feeling of the countryside, I took fewer trips. But when I did travel, I went to places most people outside of Japan don't know about. This included prefectures such as Shiga, Yamaguchi, and Ehime and towns such as Yanai, Oshima Island, and Shimonoseki. Exploring castles, hiking mountains, and getting lost in search of waterfalls consumed my weekends.

The cultural shift from Italy to Japan was a total reversal in every imaginable way. Gone were my days of driving fast and furious; if I wanted speed, I had to get on the Shinkansen. At work, the urgency and pace of things were turned up exponentially compared to Italy. There was a constant microscope on me, but with that came the opportunity to make changes in my career. Being the last to arrive, ranking higher than my boss, and having to fill the shoes of the legendary orthodontist (who had built the clinic from the ground up) I was replacing, all came with anxiety, nervousness, and excitement. I had increased responsibility but also more opportunities to shine.

When I arrived in Japan, the world was reeling from the COVID-19 pandemic, and I connected with a woman named Erin through a mutual friend. Erin had arrived two weeks before I had and was also feeling like a fish out of water. I found it incredibly helpful to have someone with whom I could bounce around ideas, vent, and share information.

Moving out to the countryside meant fewer options for homes and more challenges in fitting furniture. The Japanese don't use external lifts, so if something can't fit in the tiny doorway entrance or elevator, it's given away on the spot. I ran into this problem with a few pieces of furniture and was grateful to have been able to store them at a friend's house nearby.

The Japanese, like the Italians, value their possessions and take care of their homes, yet they are minimalists to a whole new level. Everything must have a purpose, otherwise, it has to go.

My 1076-square-foot home was the same size that entire families of four or five commonly live in. The shoe closet entrance, which I filled with all my shoes, was the same sized space my neighbor and her two kids shared.

To have a job and be able to live this lifestyle was a blessing, and I was grateful daily. The back-to-back overseas move was not planned or something I asked for, but I trusted it was where I was supposed to be.

(At Kikko Park, during Sakura (cherry blossom season) in Iwakuni, Japan — Photo by Tana Lee Photography)

Advice

Reflecting on my life BC (before Covid), I've learned that memories never leave us—they just sometimes get out of reach. As seasons come and go, you notice time passes, and change truly happens.

Reflecting on my time living and working overseas, I realized my mindset, personality, and routine had to adjust and change. Personality—a combination of skills, habits, emotions, perspectives, experiences, and hardships all blended into one—is built from patterns of behavior over an extended period of time. It can be strongly influenced by your environment, your upbringing, the people you surround yourself with, where you went to school, and more. And I was forced to shift with each new move.

Being resilient is key in the military and life overseas. And I never dreamed how much my resiliency would be challenged until what happened to me next.

CHAPTER 12: PANDEMIC IN ITALY

Timeline
Chapter 12

2020

In March, the Prime Minister of Italy issued a country-wide stay-at-home order.

In May, many restrictions were gradually eased.

In July, I was notified to be ready to move.

In September, I moved from Sicily to Japan.

In October, Italy was hit by a second wave of the pandemic, which forced the government to introduce further restrictions on movement and social life that lasted through the middle of the following year.

On March 9, 2020, the prime minister of Italy issued a stay-at-home quarantine for the entire country. Over 60 million people were told not to leave their homes except for work or emergencies.

It was like a bomb went off but you never heard it detonate. The loud, vibrant country was suddenly dead quiet. No children playing, no families talking, no church bells chiming. It was unnerving. The normal sounds of life were replaced by the screams of ambulances, police cars, and helicopters on patrol.

I felt like I was in a scary movie but didn't know when I would wake up.

Everywhere I went I had to carry a piece of paper proving who I was and why I was not quarantined at home. This document changed weekly, if not daily, because of the confusion surrounding the spread of the virus and its needing to go through the red tape of both the US and Italian governments. It was hard to keep up with the growing number of changes.

The new vocabulary of "social distancing" inserted itself into our lexicon, and then came wearing masks. It was an eerie, quiet period to live in Italy, and I was grateful for the days I was allowed to go to work to break up the monotony of quarantine.

Going to the grocery store felt like stepping into a war-torn period of the past. At first, I walked to a local fruit and vegetable stand over a mile away to purposely give myself more time outside, until one day it was closed indefinitely. When that happened, I walked down to the local supermarket and stood in the line that formed outside, waiting my turn to enter six feet apart from other patrons. A 10-minute chore was now a 2-hour expedition.

Finally my turn, I went looking for eggs, flour, and pasta—all gone. The shelves were barren as if they hadn't been restocked for weeks. The simple gesture of a smile that could barely be made out from under a mask was the only gift I could offer the clerk on my way out.

My world had changed, and I didn't know when I would be able to feel normal again. A yoga mat and YouTube became my personal gym; I knew I needed a routine to keep up my self-care. Moving my body, enriching my mind, and keeping my soul bright during this dark time had to be a priority.

Every day I also reached out to three people to catch up, connect, or do a live workout class together from our own homes. I used wine bottles as weights, paper plates as sliders, and towels as stretch assisters. Since no one was allowed to enter the country, planes stopped delivering. That meant many of the resources I took for granted were no longer an option. Bye-bye, Amazon.

When you learn to appreciate everything you have, you realize that you have everything you need.

Taking every precaution to protect my health and well-being, I watched on the news about the mobilization of the national guard and the US Naval Hospital ships with 1000 beds arriving in NYC. I kept telling myself that we will get through this together, emerge stronger, and grow more resilient. To keep sane, I made a point to go outside to listen to the wind run through the leaves and feel the sunshine hit my skin, even if for just a few minutes.

Even though I knew we would prevail as a nation and world, I feared that the virus could destroy some of us mentally even if not physically, so I knew that protecting my mental health, finding peace, and keeping a positive perspective was key. Anger never makes a situation better. Make sure worrying about tomorrow doesn't rob you of today.

It was hard not to get bogged down by the devastating impact the virus was having on Italy. On TV I watched military trucks take bodies in boxes stacked up high. All dead from COVID-19. They were being driven away to be buried. There was no room in hospitals or morgues. There was no time for (or ability to have) funerals. Families had no time to grieve, no time to say goodbye. People who contracted the virus were isolated and had to die utterly alone.

Northern Italy took the brunt of the pandemic. The virus had spread at alarming rates inside the factories. I gasped in horror when I learned entire towns were wiped out—gone. Everyone who had lived there was dead.

After Japan, Italy had the second largest population group of senior citizens, the most vulnerable group. In Italy, especially in Sicily, it was normal for three generations to live together. Italians are friendly, affectionate people who love to kiss cheeks, hold hands, and hug often. That was put on hold to slow the spread of the virus, and I could tell it was crippling for many to be forbidden from human touch, usually such a source of comfort and communication.

Schools were closed completely. Even though children were less likely to get sick and die from COVID, they could be asymptomatic carriers and bring it home to their parents and grandparents. Virtual learning took on a new meaning, and in poorer regions of the country, their lack of resources became a hindrance for all kids to stay on track.

I prayed the Italians would be able to recover. With no tourism, no stimulus checks, and no ability to work, many family businesses were forced to close. At the military base, I was grateful to be able to participate in food drives to help our host country and neighbors.

To be a productivity ninja was my goal during the pandemic. I was assisted by creating a morning routine that acted as emotional armor to protect and set me up for my day no matter what came. When I consistently practiced my morning routine, I felt protected, safe, and energized for whatever the day brought.

First thing in the morning, I would open up YouTube and follow along with a workout on my yoga mat that my friend Vanessa had sent me from her barre class. After that, I would journal, read, and then meal prep for the day. Whenever I needed a break I would stand outside on my balcony and take in the view of the ocean or Mt. Etna. On the weekdays I didn't go into work I would focus on my TED talk speech, envisioning the world healed and recovered and back to normal.

On Monday, Wednesday, and Friday evenings, I would join my Texas buddies to be pushed by our friend Cody in his virtual abs classes. It's amazing what a set of paper plates can do as sliders on a tile floor. I needed this time to recharge so I could take on the following day by storm too. My evening routine forced me to relax but also gave me the satisfaction of knowing what needed to be done was done.

One day early on in the outbreak, my dental assistant broke down crying out of immense fear that she would bring the virus home to her family. At that moment, it hit me: no matter how hard I worked, no matter how much I exercised, no matter what I did, I could also fall victim to the virus. My superpower strength was not enough.

So, we drastically changed our schedule and ensured my assistant didn't have to be in the room when I was seeing patients. Instead of greeting others with hugs, we hit elbows. Discussions for new cases with colleagues or parents now happened with six feet or more between everyone.

We started wearing N95 masks at all times, and I often felt out of breath because of them. And I began seeing the formation of marks and dark lines across my face. Because of the decreased amount of oxygen and the muffling of my voice through the mask, I often felt like I was shouting and sounding like the teacher from the Charlie Brown cartoons.

The way I practiced dentistry, the number of patients I treated, and the personal protective equipment I wore changed overnight. Some of my colleagues joked that we looked like we were going into space. For me, I often felt that my patients couldn't hear me fully or see the depth of care and emotion that I had for them and their treatment.

Suddenly, we were all living in isolated bubbles. Our expressions were masked. The social fabric of society was ripping at the seams. We all clung to any form of hope of getting back to the world we had before.

On the bright side, I was grateful to see more handwashing across the board in all sectors of society. In Sicily, they also stepped up cleaning and sanitizing procedures for bathrooms (you don't want to know what they looked like before) and other public spaces. And in May, some restrictions started being lifted.

In July 2020, I was notified to be ready to move. Then, in September, right in the middle of a global pandemic and just before a second wave would ravage Italy again, I transferred from Sicily to Japan and felt completely overwhelmed.

You would think that a military brat turned officer who has moved what felt like a thousand times would be a calm seasoned pro. But this time it felt different. From one side of the planet to the other, cultures, commands, and lifestyles could not be more different. Plus, I would have to make do without my personal items for six months because they were completely backlogged on moves that had come to a screeching halt for three months as the world reeled with the spread of the disease. Plus, my items were traveling halfway around the globe.

How did you uproot your life with so much uncertainty?

As one friend of mine said, "Focus on what you need every day and let the movers move the rest. If they lose it, it's just stuff. It's all replaceable."

She was right.

And as the French say, "C'est la vie."

That's life.

I had to sell my car, find temporary housing, and share many tearful goodbyes. But it all worked out. There were lots of speed bumps along the way, but I survived. Sometimes I found myself on edge and my emotions ran high, but I would catch myself and remember it was normal and I could take a beat.

I've heard in life that the three most stressful things you can do are change jobs, move to a new location, and add someone to the family unit. I've done the first two almost every two years my entire life, but a back-to-back overseas move upped the ante of uncertainty. As upbeat and positive as I am, I'm only human too. I have as many great days and as many shitastic days as anyone else.

But your mind can only hold one of two thoughts: a positive or a negative. You might as well fill it with positive ones. We all got here putting in the time, hard work, and energy. We are not alone, we are in this together.

During the pandemic, I found myself listening to more and more podcasts. As a social butterfly and super extrovert, I missed going out with friends, taking trips, and enjoying long meals with others. So, I found podcasts to be a worthy substitute. I listened to be enlightened and inspired. I listened to learn and think differently about things.

Stories about resilience, perseverance, struggles, and how to overcome tough times flooded my ears as I cleaned, organized, and cooked. I basked in the time I had, knowing that it was a gift to reflect, learn, and re-evaluate my life and priorities. It was a great time to think through what was best for me.

Speaking of cooking, once you find the power within you, you can change your life. The hardest part is often taking the first step. For years I avoided cooking. My parents were both wonderful chefs who loved making home-cooked meals. While in Italy, with no family, no meal prep services, and no pageant competitions coming up, I was forced to do all my own food prep and cooking. I didn't want to rely on takeout in a country famous for its wine, pasta, pizza, and gelato everywhere. But in my first week of meal prep, I struggled and felt like I was in the kitchen forever. I kept thinking, "How is this going to save me time?"

Six weeks later, however, I noticed my skin looked better, my body had more energy, and I was wasting less food and money. A year later, I started to feel out of sync if I didn't prepare my own food. With practice, it became effortless and a savior when I went back to working full-time in the clinic for 10 hours a day.

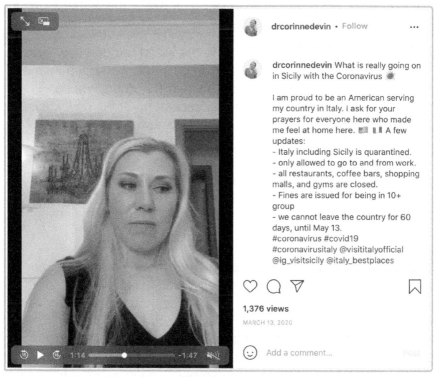

(Screenshot from a March 9, 2020's Instagram post during my first day in quarantine at my home in Catania, Italy, Sicily)

Advice

Living overseas often means seeing the world through new eyes. During the pandemic, I witnessed the best and worst of humanity. I found compassion, empathy, and respect for others whose opinions differ from mine. It can be fascinating at the new ideas you see when you open your thought process to new ways and approaches.

I was also reminded that a great life is full of people who share the same values and vision of the world with whom you can grow and learn. Together we can survive any storm and overcome any obstacle thrown our way.

Life is a fight for what you want, so if you stop fighting for your desires, what you don't want will take over. In life, we fight for integrity, character, good reputation, goals, and dreams, but if we give up hope and stop fighting to achieve these lofty goals, depression, anxiety, and hopelessness will set in. During this unprecedented time, I kept telling myself, "Stop letting things derail you, keep thinking positive, and you only lose when you quit."

In my hamster wheel of constantly moving and going nonstop, with a calendar jam-packed with trips, events, and soirees, I was forced to come to a screeching halt. A halt to rest, relax, and refocus on what was important. Very often I sacrificed sleep for gym workouts. I used to put off completing important projects like speaking at a TED talk and writing a book to go on weekend trips. I always told myself I would do them when I had time, but now that I suddenly did have time on my hands, how I was going to use it?

Your self-care is linked to your self-worth. It is up to you to find your purpose and build your resilience and tenacity. It is your job to take care of your body. It is up to you to maintain the clarity and focus you need to sustain the quality of your life.

Your life is a physical manifestation of the words running through your mind and the conversation going on in your head. You cannot have a life in the castle if your mindset is stuck in the doghouse.

Quarantine handed us a unique gift to spend more time with our families and to work on the projects or goals we never felt we had time to achieve. We were all grounded, on deployment as my military friends would say, except we got to sleep in our own beds and watch Netflix whenever we wanted.

But what good can come from being a lazy couch potato, especially with such a unique set of circumstances laid out for the healthy? I felt I needed to rise up and focus on the personal growth I could accomplish from the safety of my home. I knew we as a human race would persevere past this challenge and this quarantine wouldn't last forever. How could I make the most of it?

I immediately started reaching out to speaker coaches and eventually met Kymberlee. She was thoughtful, kind, patient, and engaging. For an hour every week, we met to develop my story, my talk, and my gift to the world in speech form. She taught me how to tell stories to spread my message, and when the doors of the TEDx events open, I would be ready.

No one imagined the pandemic to last as long as it did, and I pray that when this book is published, we will all be laughing about the silly things we complained about.

So what did we learn?

How did our mindset and focus change?

What areas in our lives did we previously ignore but now need to examine closely?

If you are still, if you do nothing, if you do not move forward, the truth of that matter is that you have quit. Yet, at the same time, if you are an overachiever like I am, you may need to come to terms with how much is on your plate. I loved staying busy and doing it all, but I realized you can't do everything all at once. You have to choose. You have to prioritize. You have to ask for help and not be afraid to keep asking for help until you get it. I'm far more resourceful and resilient than I knew, which has led me to develop relationships with new people who opened my eyes and helped me grow.

To be fully present means to let go.

COVID-19 has reminded me just how interconnected we truly are. The virus doesn't care where you come from, the color of your skin, who you voted for, or where you live. It is an invisible enemy that brought a time of unprecedented change. Healthcare will be revolutionized into a more patient-centered model.

One of the most healing and empowering perspectives to take is to recognize that what has occurred in the past has prepared me for today, for this point in my life. Many of us feel like our life is on hold and parts of it may be, but how is that different when we were in school, traveling the world, or at home recovering from an illness?

If we can look back at our lives, connect the dots, and find the nuggets of wisdom left behind by experience, we can see insight into how to change patterns, show up differently, and be more compassionate humans.

Take all that you have learned and pulled it into this moment here and now. You can be the person you always wanted to be. It just requires a bit of courage to take the first step.

"Veni. Vidi. Vici." I came. I saw. I conquered.

That is how you should look at every single day because it's a gift whether it was amazing or it didn't go quite the way you planned. That's life. Many things are out of our control. And no matter what you do today when you wake up tomorrow, it's a brand new day to start over anew.

Just focus on your dreams and goals. When you protect your purpose, your purpose protects you. How we all get to where we are in life is from a complex sequence of events. Cherish that thought. It's too complicated to map out minute to minute, so make the best decision you can at the time and enjoy riding the wave as things unfold.

Life is beautiful, messy, and always veering off from the plan. The truth is we have no idea what life has in store for us.

CHAPTER 13: FORGING AHEAD— LEAD LIKE A QUEEN

Activity
Checklist

1	Find Your Dream and Set Your Goals
2	Identify Your Word for the Year
3	Leverage Teamwork and Help from Others
4	Work Through "Failure"
5	Magnify Your Mantras
6	Celebrate, Prioritize Self-Care, and Pause the People Pleasing
7	Stick To A Morning Routine
8	Work At Getting Past "No"
9	Learn From Me: What I Wish I Knew When I Was Younger
10	Elevate the Right Relationships
11	Develop Your Leadership
12	Steer Clear of Comfortable
13	Overcome Fear

The most frequently asked question I get when it comes to balancing my life and 'doing it all' is: "Corinne, how are you able to look chaos in the face and tell it to knock it off?"

My answer is simpler than people think: "Make a list."

I realized early on that we all need reminders and ways to hold ourselves accountable to stay on track. For me, making yearly and daily goals in list form helps me pursue my purpose. As I make small steps toward the goals each day, I check them off one by one —and they add up to big success. Lists are my secret to excelling in life.

My wish for you as you read this final chapter is that I have shared some inspiration and will give you my parting words here to anyone who has ever felt inferior, disadvantaged, or lost in life.

The voyage through life is rarely smooth sailing. We all stumble, we all have setbacks, and we all have obstacles that we encounter whether it's in our business, our personal lives, or our careers.

Challenges, failure, and learning will happen. When it does, just remember that if you don't quit, you cannot fail.

I encourage you to go through each of the 13 activities in the list below at least once, and then return to sections you need more practice with again and again until you achieve mastery.

"Always remember you are braver than you believe, stronger than you seem, smarter than you think, and twice as beautiful as you've ever imagined."—Dr. Seuss

1. Find Your Dream and Set Your Goals

Step 1: Write down everything that you're chasing right now.
Don't hold back, don't edit, don't analyze. Write it all down.

Step 2: Ask yourself the following questions.
- Where did these ideas come from?
- Is this really my dream? (Or am I chasing someone else's?)

- What's my passion?
- What's my purpose?
- What makes me excited to play this game called life?

No alarm clock needed—what wakes you up in the morning with drive and determination? Do you eat, drink, and sleep it?

What makes a difference in the quality of your life? What helps you break through obstacles? Do you have to achieve and expand? If you have this, you will find an answer to any problem.

If one day you wake up and realize that being mediocre sucks and being average sucks, you'll start moving. Then, keep going no matter how many times you get knocked down.

If you are like most people, you usually have more than one goal. Drive, ambition, and focus only get you so far. Goals are just dreams until you write them down. I both write mine down and also look at them in my office and at home every day.

Write your goals down now.

It's fun to dream about what life will be like once your goals are accomplished. Yet, it is easy to get distracted when you have a tough week at work or something goes awry in your personal life. Committed action, not just dreaming, is required to reach them.

Step 3: Make sure your goals are written down and written correctly.
It's important to make your goals specific, measurable, and realistic. This way you will know when you are making progress, which will give you the motivation to complete them.

For example, I often hear people say, "I want to lose weight."

However, this is not specific enough. Instead, if your goal were to be, "I will lose 10 pounds in three months," now you have a specific, measurable, and realistic goal.

Another example you may have is, "I want to save money or pay off debt."

This too is not clear enough or measurable. Instead, make it something like, "I will save $5,000 and pay off my $3,500 credit card debt by December 31st."

A third example you may have written down is, "I want to be a billionaire and retire by age 35."

This could be quite unrealistic if you are currently 30 years old, in debt, and with bad money management habits that need adjusting.

Step 4: Take action immediately.
Once a goal is specific, measurable, and realistic, your brain will get to work figuring out the steps to get you there. Make sure to take action, even if very small, right away.

With a financial goal, for example, you might create an Excel spreadsheet to mathematically calculate your monthly savings rate, make a budget, and cut back on joyless spending to divert funds into paying down debt, building up an emergency fund, or investing for compounding growth.

Step 5: Self-Check: Do Your Words Match Your Actions?
To achieve our goals, we need to create new habits and stick to them. A small action every day can pay dividends over time. It's not enough to say you want something; you have to act in a way that moves you in the right direction.

Don't just say that you want to save more money, start cooking or baking your favorite meals at home rather than eating out so often.

Don't just say you want to be in better shape, start walking and biking to places instead of driving or join a workout class for accountability.

Note:
At certain times of the year, some goals will take more priority than others. While some necessitate daily action and others do not, both types of goals require discipline and consistency.

If you work hard, you can accomplish anything.

2. Identify Your Word for the Year

An exercise you can try—that has helped me achieve my goals and stay focused over the years—is to pick a word theme for your yearly goals. It keeps you grounded. The word for the year can be anything that aligns with your focus and intentions.

Here are a few ideas:
- peace
- connect
- align
- present
- intentional
- purpose
- adventure
- movement

How do I find my word?

We all have people we listen to, follow, read, or watch who make us feel good, inspire us, and motivate us when we are down.

So, if you don't know where to find your word, start by listening to and reading some of your favorite people to help your brain generate ideas.

Another way is to clear your mind. Go for a walk, work out, do some meditation, or take a long shower. These are great ways to help you physically and mentally relax. In this state, you are more likely to feel drawn to a word that captures your intentions.

Then what?

Once you feel confident in one word that will remind you of your goals and focus of the year, break your goals down into categories.

If we think of all the categories in life where we have goals and break them down then it becomes easier for us to narrow our focus on each area and not get overwhelmed with everything we want to do and accomplish in our year. Not every category needs to be grand and complex.

For example, you could have a category called "Relationships." Your goal could be to learn how to take a compliment with grace or how to communicate better.

You could also have a category called "Speaking." Your goal could be to overcome your fear of public speaking by getting comfortable and confident in front of five or fewer people.

Whatever you choose for categories and goals, make them things that will push you to grow and move you one step closer to being better today than yesterday.

For example, here were my categories for 2022:
1. Relationships
2. Speaking
3. Writing
4. Fitness
5. Finance
6. Makeup
7. Website
8. Business
9. Social Media

What are your categories?

3. Leverage Teamwork and Help from Others

Everybody in this world wants something — greatness, excellence, recognition — but the questions are:
- What am I willing to go through to get it?
- Am I dedicated?
- Am I ready to sacrifice?
- Am I disciplined?
- What type of commitment am I willing to give?
- Are my thoughts and behaviors constructive or destructive?
- What would I do today if I knew I would not fail?

Achieving big things should be a challenge, but if you are smart, you'll use collaboration and teamwork to make win-wins for all involved.

As the African proverb says, "If you want to go far, go together."

We cannot accomplish big goals alone. We need partners, mentors, coaches, or even tutors to get us there. It's okay to get help.

No successful person you know got to the place that you admire without failures, learning from mistakes, and lots of help from others. The path to success isn't easy. It's often a bumpy road with detours and stop signs that come out of nowhere, but the journey is worth it.

Pro Tips:
- Work with a master to go faster.
- Build a team of others who believe in your vision.

4. Work Through "Failure"

If it's not challenging you, it's not changing you. Although it's never too late to pursue your passions and live them out, you will hit obstacles along the way.

Find joy even in the small progress you make toward your goal. Noticing small changes will motivate you to keep going. And if you stumble or take a detour, just get back on track. How we rebound is far more important than the fact that we fell.

If you do "fail," here are a few good things to say to yourself:
- All I've got is my "A game," let's go again.
- You will not outwork me.
- I am willing to earn it.
- I put in the effort to get where I'm at today.
- I won't lose my competitive edge—I'll get it back.
- If I want the success others have paid for in blood, sweat, and tears, I have to be willing to pay full price for it too.
- Action cures fear.

- I will overcome this.
- Be a light in this world.
- Strive for progress, not perfection.
- I must believe in myself first—others will follow.

If you want a happy and fulfilled life, then consistently ask yourself, "Is this contributing to a good life? Is it helping me grow?"

If not, cut it out and get back on course.

You are either moving forward or backward. Be conscious of the content you consume and the 'audiotape' you let run in your head.

Cut out negative self-talk, replace it with positive thinking, and get back into action.

I will find a way, honor my truth, and keep pursuing my dreams through thick and thin. Rain or shine, I will march on.

5. Magnify Your Mantras

My mantra is: "You've got this."

Now it's your turn. Think about what your mantra could be and what you will do with it to strive toward a magnificent life.

As you develop your mantra, think about what words fill your thoughts in a moment of weakness. When you are searching for strength, these are the words that will help get you to the next level.

Your mantra will bring you peace, tranquility, and a feeling of calm as it reminds you of your inner greatness.

Sometimes we need that reminder. And, if it helps, imagine your mantra coming from a mentor, coach, family member, friend, or anyone you admire.

Dream more, complain less.
Listen more, talk less.

COMMANDER TO CROWN

Love more, argue less.
Hope more, fear less.
Relax more, worry less.
Believe more, doubt less.
Play more, work less.

Monitor your energy and be mindful of whom you give your time to and the people you surround yourself with.

Learn to say no. It can feel great to say yes in the moment, but when you say no to one thing in your life, you are saying yes to something else. And vice versa. Choose wisely.

Show me your friends, and I will show you your future. This is true in every aspect of our lives.

Train your mind to see the good in every situation.

Know the value you bring and don't accept less than you're worth.

Contribute to others. This need not be financial. Give a hug, share a compliment, advise a friend, help a stranger, or donate time to feed the less fortunate.

We build confidence with integrity.

The most important relationship we have in life is with ourselves.

The most important things are often the hardest to say.

Every morning you have two choices: continue to sleep with your dreams or get up and chase them.

Your mind can only think one thought at a time. Therefore, if you're thinking of something helpful or positive, you cannot think of something hurtful or negative too. Fill your head with helpful, proactive thoughts.

Where you started is not where you'll finish. Who do you need to become to achieve your goals? That must be your focus.

Stop looking for red flags as excuses to procrastinate and start looking for green lights. Go!

"Our life is what our thoughts make it."—Marcus Aurelius.

There are no accidents in God's universe.

Successful people keep moving. They make mistakes but don't quit.

Know what you believe, write down your goals, and review them daily.

Thoughts and beliefs are reinforced over time. Visualize achieving your goals.

Wearing masks—because of the pandemic—may feel like a disconnect from others, but masks don't cover your eyes, which show the strength of your soul.

Life is meant to be lived—now. If you are not happy, then change, shift gears, and take a chance.

If what you are doing doesn't make you fully alive and express your real goals, then stop.

If you know in your heart that you are going after the right goals, then go all in, be resilient, and strive relentlessly for your dreams.

Keep marching on. Get past the hurt, the anger, the disappointment, the shame, the struggle, the regret, the embarrassment—and keep marching on. You will be a successful person.

Times are changing, be optimistic. Tough times will pass.

Believe that change is possible.

Create habits that set you up for success, including keystone habits that create a culture change or a paradigm shift.

To break the rules, you must first master them.

When you have grit, you will strenuously work toward challenges. You will maintain interest and effort over the years despite failures, setbacks, adversity, and plateaus. What is most interesting is how grit emerges—through consistency, mental strength, and discipline.

Sometimes the worst things in life can be the greatest blessing.

We were meant to explore and step into the unknown.

Be strong, be fearless, be beautiful.

Believe that anything is possible when you have the right people there to support you.

6. Celebrate, Prioritize Self-Care, and Pause the People Pleasing

With any large goal, task, or project that you finish, it is important to celebrate in the moment. Then, give yourself time and space to reset.

Give yourself permission to enjoy a small victory and catch your breath. If you don't, it will catch up to you.

I've noticed when I keep going like the energizer bunny, I become forgetful about small things and more tired than normal. Your mind and body need to shut down sometimes as if the batteries needed to be recharged. This is when you need to prioritize self-care.

Never underestimate what a good night's rest, a workout, or a good meal can do. A bad diet can't be erased by exercise. Poor habits can't be rehabilitated instantly into good ones.

When others around you start seeing the changes you make, they'll notice that you walk differently, hold your head up a bit higher, and have a spirit inside you that shines. They will want a piece of it.

They will come to you, wanting to spend time with you and seek your counsel. Yet, sometimes this can deplete you.

I say this as a recovering people pleaser. When I was younger, I would help others even at my own expense because I wanted to be seen as a "good girl" and not let anyone down. As much as we all want to lean in and be perfect for everyone in every way, something has to give. We need to take care of ourselves first before we give a piece of that to others.

7. Stick To A Morning Routine

I believe a morning routine is key. It's like putting on emotional armor to protect yourself from the battlefield of life, full of conflicts and fires you have to put out each day.

Your routine is something you do for yourself that makes you feel good. I do things for both my body and my mind so that I feel ready for whatever comes at me next.

Here's my morning routine:
1. Wake up by 4:00 am
   - (subtract two hours from when you need to be at your office)
2. Go to the gym for 60 minutes
   - (this gives you a full hour to do weights, cardio, yoga, stretching, meditation, or whatever you need to start your day)
3. State three things I'm grateful for out loud
4. Review my three biggest challenges for the day
   - (I write these out the night before)
5. Tackle my top three priorities
   - (circle or underline what these are to keep your mind focused on what you need to do)

Very often we push aside the things we need to do and focus on something else instead. Rather than procrastinate, tackle the toughest and most challenging items first when you are fresh and focused. That way it builds momentum to do other things.

For example, while writing and editing this book, I focused on it in the morning when I was the freshest and before I let anything else de-prioritize it. So I found a quiet place with wifi and spent time on the book first. Afterward, I always felt like the rest of my day was off to a great start. Tackling your top priorities makes you feel terrific and like a huge weight is lifted off your shoulders.

When you craft an environment to succeed, you set yourself up for success.

What is your morning routine?

8. Work At Getting Past "No"

I've encountered many obstacles when needing to do something for my patients, colleagues, or clinic seems impossible—especially when leaders have said, "no."

But, as Marie Forleo would say, I've learned that everything is figure-out-able.

When you know your audience, it will better equip you for turning no into yes. Do some research to figure out:
- What are their reasons for saying no?
- What are their concerns?
- Are there rules or instructions to go by?
- How can I make this a win-win?

In the military, we have tons of guidelines and standard practices. Understanding them is key to getting through to your leaders. If you can dispel concerns, counter arguments, and back up your plan with past precedent and logical reasoning, you can get from no to yes far easier.

Sure, sometimes people are power hungry, but reputation matters. What goes around, comes around. Life has a funny way of circling back onto others who have shown poor leadership, so do not fret. Do your best, make your case, and move forward no matter the decision handed down.

"What is for you will not miss you. God's rejection is His protection."—Kellie Hall

9. Learn From Me: What I Wish I Knew When I Was Younger

Never let anybody make you feel bad about the results you've worked your butt off to achieve. Don't lose sleep over haters. The reason they have a problem with your life is that they have no life themselves. Hurt people hurt people. Eliminate people and situations from your life that bring you problems, drama, negativity, and dysfunction.

It's not about today, it's about the future. Easy never pays well. It takes real time and commitment every day to achieve worthwhile things. Focus and commit to working hard every day for 10 years to be great. There's no quick easy way to get there.

What you think is important in adolescence doesn't hold true in life as an adult. As you get older, what others think matters less. What you think is what's important.

Education is your passport in life, but school doesn't stop after you get your degree or leave the classroom. You are forever evolving. Your mind needs constant stimulation to grow and keep learning.

Let go of your pride. Growing up in a military family on military bases, I wore my pride like a badge of honor. I was taught at a young age to hide my feelings and that it's okay to feel scared just never let it show. Fake it until you make it.

However, when you don't let people see you for who you really are, it makes for a superficial connection. It wasn't until I went on deployment that I was forced to hit the reset button in order to give and receive complete trust with my unit and battle buddy friendships. When you let your guard down, admit when you screw up, and say how you will fix it, people respect you more.

10. Elevate the Right Relationships

In a world where you can have a million friends validate you on social media, who will truly be there when you need them? Even when you are thousands of miles, several oceans, and time zones apart, technology has increased our ability to communicate with friends and family like never before. When you respect, trust, and love someone from a distance, you can deepen your bond and be absolutely unstoppable when you're together.

But are you willing to make these relationships a priority? We all have people in our lives who we love but do not always communicate with regularly. That's okay. Perhaps they don't like talking on the phone or sending emails. Perhaps they can't figure out video conferencing. Nevertheless, when you meet up in person or know you will both be in the same area, it's as if all time has stopped and you can pick up where you left off.

What I've learned growing up in the military is when you are focused on the past, you are blind to your present. What is your story? What is their story? How are you part of each other's stories?

Look at each relationship you maintain. Does the other person support you or weigh you down? Will he or she add positive energy or toxicity to your life? Every friendship and every relationship ebbs and flows, and it's up to you to decide if it's worth putting in the effort or letting it be a lovely memory.

Be around the light bringers, magic makers, world shifters, and game shakers. They challenge you. They break you open, uplift you, and expand you. They don't let you play small with your life.

These heartbeats are your people. These people are your tribe.

11. Develop Your Leadership

There are many hard things you must do if you want to be a successful leader. When trouble comes your way, consider it an opportunity for greatness. Your faith will be tested by challenges and obstacles. You have to be able to keep an eye on the future but stay focused on the present.

You have to be able to reach your goals and deliver on results. Get comfortable with being uncomfortable. Feel the fear and take the risk anyway. Inspire others while finding your own motivation. Find effective easy to bring people along when they're reluctant to move forward.

Rise above drama and dysfunction.

Embrace failure as you fail forward. Be accountable for your actions and take responsibility for your behavior.

You have to trust before you can be trusted.

Lead by example even when there is no path. Be positive, even if everyone else goes negative. Lead, even if no one else is following.

Care about others, maybe more than they care about you.

Concern yourself more about your character than your reputation.

Ask questions even though people don't always have answers.

You have to invest in yourself even though others may not invest in you or even themselves.

When it comes to being a strong woman: know it, own it, be it, and then support those around you who embody the same mindset. Every day is a chance to celebrate women. I feel so fortunate to be surrounded by the most badass, hard-working, relentless women who do everything with both passion and grace.

Every person you admire, aspire to be like, and put on a pedestal is just a regular person like you who has worked their butt off. You've got to go all in. Successful people are consistent, they have learned to develop their mindset and do it again and again, slightly better each time.

The bolder and more courageous you are now, the bolder and more courageous you will be in the future.

The more confident you are today, the more confident you will be in the future.

The more obstacles you can overcome today, the bigger obstacles you will be able to overcome tomorrow.

Wherever focus goes, energy flows. Know your path beyond knowing it. Narrow your focus, make it a priority, and stay there no matter what. You must know it blindly. Clarity is power, and the clearer vision you have about exactly what you want with your goals, your brain will go there and find solutions to get you closer.

We do not retreat, we do not give up, and we do not surrender.

The reason why most are not successful is that every time stuff does not go their way, they give up, they quit, and they let go. Other people can sense that weakness. You can feel when someone's not fully committed—when they are not all-in.

Staying average is a weak mentality. We must believe so much that we're arrogant about it. Go hard in school, the gym, your career, and your life.

12. Steer Clear of Comfortable

Tell me one great thing in your life that came as a result of being comfortable. Can you think of anything? I can't.

Yet everywhere I look in today's society, people are doing all that they can to be more comfortable. They're looking for more convenience, they're looking for quick answers, they're looking for fast results, and they're looking for an unearned path to greatness.

All the successful people that you look up to are successful because they find joy in being uncomfortable. When you try to avoid the pain, to avoid the struggle, to avoid the hard things, you are actively choosing to be average, you are actively choosing to be mediocre, and you are actively choosing to move further away from what you want in life.

Hardships, pain, and struggle give you the skills, mindset, and tools that forge you into a champion.

Processes that build up to success are always inconvenient at first, but if you stick with them, give them time, and work through them, they become habits that are easily done with passive effort and little thought.

Create automatic actions in your life and create automatic winning.

It's easy to lose faith and lose heart in the things you want to do. Do not define yourself by your expectations. Life is full of change, that's the only certain thing. So, protect your dream, but don't let it limit you. Make sure what you're striving for is something that you love. If not, it's not worth it.

Life has an interesting way of opening a new path that you couldn't have expected.

Be kind, have empathy, and show gratitude every single day. What you do today shapes who you are tomorrow. Be strategically focused, have a work-life balance that works for you, and come up with constructive solutions to change situations for the better.

Deliver a positive message of courage, vision, fortitude, patience, and persistence.

"You have brains in your head. You have feet in your shoes. You can steer yourself in any direction you choose." — Dr. Seuss

Take chances to go outside the box. This is an opportunity, this can be a rebirth. You only live once, so do what you are passionate about.

Make up your mind and don't let people talk you out of it, don't let circumstances discourage you, and don't let delays get in your way. You have to stay focused on your goal.

Did something throw you off course? Well, find something to throw you back on.

When you decide to do something, you flip the frequency in your brain to do something right now. You don't need to know how you are going to do it, you just need to know you are going to do it.

There's always going to be a reason if you want it badly enough.

13. Overcome Fear

Often the biggest challenge we face is getting past ourselves. When we combine uncertainty and anxiety, we get fear. We can step into our fear with our body's response of flight or fight and choose to fight, automatically. We can train our brain in a way that it goes on autopilot.

When we make progress, we get hits of dopamine that feel good and motivate us to keep going. This is really powerful.

But how can I halt fear?

As you feel fear coming on, stay in your conscious thinking. Breathe, meditate, and visualize a positive, successful outcome. Focus on what you can control in your environment.

For example, if your fear is public speaking, you can practice speaking in the room before you have to do it in front of an audience. Then you could do it again with a small number of trusted people to give you feedback. In this way, you are pushing yourself to overcome your fear but controlling the progression one step at a time versus being overwhelmed by the entire staircase.

When you feel you are in control it will allow you to feel grounded and thereby give you certainty. Learning to do this habitually will move you towards your goals and away from your fears.

"To accomplish great things, we must not only act, but also dream; not only plan, but also believe." —Anatole France

— — —

Forge ahead and lead like a Queen! I believe in you.

Corinne

(July 2018: When crowned Ms. Earth 2018 — Photo by Intuition Design Photography.)

RESOURCES

Resources
and Contact Info

Coaches

Hair & Makeup Artists and Styling

Military

Orthodontists

Pageant Systems

Photographers

Social Media and Video

About This Bonus Section

I have learned that you can grow faster, develop sooner, and reach your goals at incredible rates when you work with the best people in your field.

Below you will find a list of individuals—in alphabetical order—who are not only experts at what they do but professional and well-respected.

They are colleagues, friends, mentors, and artists who have helped me achieve my goals and dreams while balancing my career.

When we take on a new challenge it is often difficult to know where to start. So, I wanted to provide my best resources for a starting point for whom to reach out to when you are unsure how to take your first step.

The categories below include coaches, hair & makeup artists and styling, military, orthodontists, pageant systems, photographers, and social media and video.

Additionally, I would like to thank everyone on this list who permitted me to share their information.

Good luck. You got this.

Corinne

Coaches

1. Adrian Kwan
   - Email: info@ThePageantProject.com
   - Website: ThePageantProject.com

2. Alexis Landrum
   - Email: AlexisLandrum@Hotmail.com
   - Instagram: Instagram.com/Alexis.Landrum.Travel

3. Janice McQueen Ward
   - Email: JaniceMcQueenWard@gmail.com
   - Website: JaniceMcQueen.com
   - Facebook: Facebook.com/JaniceMcQueenWard
   - Instagram: Instagram.com/JaniceMcQueenWard

4. Kymberlee Weil
   - Email: hello@StorytellingSchool.com
   - Website: StorytellingSchool.com
   - Instagram: Instagram.com/StorytellingSchool
   - Podcast: StorytellingSchool.com/podcast

5. Laura Petersen—Book Writing and Self-Publishing
   - Email: Laura@CopyThatPops.com
   - Website: CopyThatPops.com
   - Facebook: Facebook.com/LauraP23
   - Instagram: Instagram.com/LaptopLaura
   - LinkedIn: Linkedin.com/in/LauraPetersen
   - Twitter: Twitter.com/LaptopLaura
   - Podcast: CopyThatPops.com/iTunes

6. Laurel House
   - Email: Laurel@LaurelHouse.com
   - Website: LaurelHouse.com
   - Instagram: Instagram.com/LaurelHouse

7. Wendi Russo
   - Email: RussoWendi@yahoo.com
   - Website: WendiRussotv.com
   - Instagram: Instagram.com/Wendi_Russo

Hair & Makeup Artists and Styling

1. Cindy Stirling
   * Website: CindyStirling.com
   * Instagram: Instagram.com/CindyStirling_muah

2. Kiss & Makeup Houston, Founder & CEO: Sandra Mata
   * Email: info@KissAndMakeupHouston.com
   * Website: KissAndMakeupHouston.com
   * Instagram: Instagram.com/KissAndMakeupHouston

3. Marc Defang
   * Website: MarcDeFang.com
   * Facebook: Facebook.com/MarcDeFang
   * Instagram: Instagram.com/MarcDeFang

4. The Perfect Face Founder & CEO: Danielle Doyle
   * Email: info@ThePerfectFace.com
   * Website: tpfcosmetics.com and ThePerfectFace.com
   * Facebook: Facebook.com/tpfcosmetics
   * Instagram: Instagram.com/ThePerfectFace
   * Twitter: Twitter.com/ThePerfectFace
   * Phone: 713-977-3223

5. UK Glam Squad, Duncan Fisher & Patti Baston
   * Email: GlamSquadUK8@gmail.com
   * Facebook: Facebook.com/GlamSquadUK8
   * Instagram: Instagram.com/UKGlamSquad

Military

1. CAPT (ret.) Scott Curtice, U.S. Navy Dental Corps, Board Certified Orthodontist
   * Phone: 619-562-5437
   * Website: SanteeKids.com

2. CDR Jeff Pietrzyk, U.S. Navy JAG Corps,
   * LinkedIn: Linkedin.com/in/BecomingSuperfly

3. Dr. Alberto Lunetta, Naval Air Station Sigonella Community Relations Director
- Email: Alberto.Lunetta.it@eu.navy.mil
- Phone: +39 335-779-0451

4. Dr. Mark Ranschart, served in the U.S. Army Dental Corps
- Email: MRanschaert@gmail.com

5. Dr. Nathan H. Carlson, DPT, MAJ, U.S. Army Reserves
- Email: ChampionRunningGroup@gmail.com
- Facebook: Facebook.com/Nathan.Carlson.96
- Instagram: Instagram.com/DrNateInsta
- Twitter: Twitter.com/Dr_Nate_Carlson

6. Dr. Payton Fennel, served in the U.S. Navy Medical Corps
- Email: sportsdoc2018@gmail.com
- LinkedIn:
  Linkedin.com/in/Payton-Fennell-do-mba-862717162

7. LT Kellie Hall, U.S. Navy, Human Resources Officer
- Instagram: Instagram.com/MissUnderstood.Podcast
- Podcast: Misunderstood with Kellie Rene Hall

8. Rebecca Ortenzio Lee, DDS, MSD, Captain, Dental Corps, USN (retired), Diplomate, American Board of Orthodontics

9. Richard McManus, Public Affairs Specialist, Luke Air Force Base, Phoenix, Arizona
- Email: McManusRichard@yahoo.com

10. Vivienne Nguyen, JD, Assistant District Attorney, served in the U.S. Navy JAG Corps
- LinkedIn: Linkedin.com/in/VivienneNguyen

Orthodontists

1. Dr. T. Carl Loeffler
- Email: tl_634@usc.edu

2. Dr. Courtney Dunn
   - Email: Courtney@WomenInOrthodontics.com
   - Website: WomenInOrthodontics.com

3. Dr. Dovi Prero, Prero Orthodontics
   - Website: PreroOrthodontics.com
   - Facebook: Facebook.com/PreroOrthodontics
   - Instagram: Instagram.com/PreroOrthodontics

4. Dr. Gerry Samson
   - Website: gnathosce.com

5. Dr. S. Jay Bowman, Kalamazoo Orthodontics
   - Email: info@KalamazooOrthodontics.com
   - Phone: 269-344-2466
   - Website: KalamazooOrthodontics.com
   - Facebook: Facebook.com/KalamazooOrthodontics

Pageant Systems

1. Earth, Director Mkyhael Michaels
   - Email: Info@MrsEarthPageant.com
   - Phone: 219-Beauty1 (219-232-8891)
   - Website: MsEarthPageant.com

2. Galaxy, Director: Maria Torres
   - Email: Maria@GalaxyPageants.com
   - Website: GalaxyPageants.com
   - Facebook: Facebook.com/GalaxyPageant

3. International Ms., Director: Laura Clark
   - Website: InternationalMsPageant.com
   - Instagram: Instagram.com/InternationalmsPageant
   - Instagram: Instagram.com/DirectorLauraClark
   - LinkedIn: Linkedin.com/in/DirectorLauraClark

4. United America, Assistant Director: Vanessa Sikorski
   - Facebook: Facebook.com/Vanessa.Sikorski.9
   - Phone: 979-229-1021

5. United States National Pageants™
- Website: UnitedStatesCrown.com
- Facebook: Facebook.com/TheUnitedStatesNationalPageants
- Instagram: Instagram.com/TheUnitedStatesPageants

Photographers

1. Arielle Levy
- Email: ArielleLevyPhoto@gmail.com
- Website: ArielleLevyPhoto.com
- Instagram: Instagram.com/ArielleLevyPhoto

2. Charlotte Clemie Photography
- Email: Info@CharlotteClemiePhotography.com
- Website: CharlotteClemiePhotography.com
- Instagram: Instagram.com/CharlotteClemiePhotographer

3. Steve Grant, GRANT FOTO Photography
- Email: info@GrantFoto.com
- Website: GrantFoto.com
- Instagram: Instagram.com/GrantFoto

4. Tana Lee Photography
- Email: TanaLeePhotography@gmail.com
- Website: TanaLeePhotography.myportfolio.com
- Instagram: Instagram.com/TanaLeePhotography

Social Media and Video

1. Patrick Stephens
- Email: Patrick@iehdProductions.com
- Phone: (909) 573-3011

2. Veronica Olivarez
- LinkedIn: Linkedin.com/in/VOlivarez

ABOUT THE
AUTHOR

DR. CORINNE DEVIN

DR. CORINNE DEVIN

PUBLIC SPEAKER & INFLUENCER

Dr. Corinne Devin: US Navy Commander, Orthodontist, Motivational Speaker, World Traveler, and International Ms. 2020.

As a multi-passionate woman, she has learned to not only balance her passions but use them to maker her a better officer.

Daughter of the American Revolution, deployed with the United States Navy in support of Operation Iraqi Freedom to Al Asad, attended the elite Tri-Service Orthodontics Residency Program at Wilford Hall Medical Center, a keynote speaker at STEM (Science Technology Engineering and Mathematics) Conference to over 1,000 middle school girls for the Department of Defense in Japan and Italy.

18	.29	50	8	67
% WOMEN IN THE US MILITARY	% OF WOMEN MAKE RANK OF COMMANDER IN THE US NAVY	COUNTRIES VISITED	PAGEANT TITLES AWARDED	MEDIA FEATURES

@DRCORINNEDEVIN | DRCORINNEDEVIN@GMAIL.COM

Corinne Devin Bio

Dr. Corinne Devin is a triple crown-holding beauty queen and a US Naval officer. She is a Navy Commander, board-certified orthodontist, and public speaker with a passion for volunteering.

While in residency, Corinne competed and won the Ms. Texas pageant. After graduating, she went on to win Ms. United States 2012, Ms. Galaxy 2014, Ms. Earth 2018, and International Ms. 2020. The titles allowed her to get more involved with local communities, speak at events, and mentor young girls, who she loves to show they can be and do anything they want – from beauty queen to Navy officer to orthodontist.

Corinne was the keynote speaker at a STEM (Science Technology Engineering and Mathematics) conference in Japan for over 1,000 middle school girls for the Department of Defense. Corinne's motivational talks have also included high schools and professional societies in Italy and the American Association of Orthodontists in the US.

In the Navy, Corinne has served at Naval Medical Center San Diego; US Naval Hospital Yokosuka, Japan; US Naval Hospital Sigonella, Italy; and Marine Corps Air Station, Iwakuni, Japan. She also deployed to Al Asad, Iraq, supporting Operation Iraqi Freedom in 2009.

Corinne believes that being well-rounded can inspire, motivate, and plant the seed of determination into our youth and their peers. Her "caring is contagious" mantra is evident in her engaging with, speaking to, and writing for future leaders as she captivates audiences everywhere.

Connect with Corinne

- Email: DrCorinneDevin@gmail.com
- Website: DrCorinneDevin.com
- Facebook: Facebook.com/DrCorinneDevin
- Instagram: Instagram.com/DrCorinneDevin
- LinkedIn: Linkedin.com/in/DrCorinneDevin
- YouTube: Youtube.com/c/DrCorinneDevin

For more, visit DrCorinneDevin.com/media to see magazines, podcasts, and other publications Corinne has been featured in.

Made in the USA
Las Vegas, NV
01 August 2022

52529329R00108